HANNAH & THE SALISH SEA

Hannah &
the Salish Sea

Carol Anne Shaw

RONSDALE PRESS

HANNAH & THE SALISH SEA
Copyright © 2013 Carol Anne Shaw

RONSDALE PRESS
3350 West 21st Avenue, Vancouver, B.C., Canada V6S 1G7
www.ronsdalepress.com

Typesetting: Julie Cochrane, in Minion 12 pt on 16
Cover Art & Design: Nancy de Brouwer, Massive Graphic Design
Paper: Ancient Forest Friendly "Silva" (FSC)—100% post-consumer waste,
    totally chlorine-free and acid-free

Ronsdale Press wishes to thank the following for their support of its publishing program: the Canada Council for the Arts, the Government of Canada through the Canada Book Fund, the British Columbia Arts Council and the Province of British Columbia through the British Columbia Book Publishing Tax Credit program.

Library and Archives Canada Cataloguing in Publication

Shaw, Carol Anne, 1960–
    Hannah & the Salish Sea / Carol Anne Shaw.

ISBN 978-1-55380-233-4 (print)
ISBN 978-1-55380-234-1 (ebook) / ISBN 978-1-55380-235-8 (pdf)

    I. Title. II. Title: Hannah and the Salish Sea.

PS8637.H3836H35 2013   jC813'.6   C2012-907712-7

At Ronsdale Press we are committed to protecting the environment. To this end we are working with Canopy (formerly Markets Initiative) and printers to phase out our use of paper produced from ancient forests. This book is one step towards that goal.

Printed in Canada by Marquis Printing, Quebec

for Richard

ACKNOWLEDGEMENTS

Writing a book is sometimes a lonely experience, and I am forever grateful to the people in my life who either give me a kick in the pants when I'm procrastinating, or pull the plug on my laptop when it's time for a break. You know who you are!

Thank you to Cameron, Dan and Selinde, and especially, Kristine, the brilliant members of my writing group, FRANK, whose honest feedback, constructive criticism and unfailing sense of humor have been as important to me as a good breakfast. You guys rock! Thanks also to my extended family for putting up with my stream-of-consciousness chatter and my bad hair days during the revision process. Your tact is noted and appreciated. Thanks as well to my grown-up lads for never failing to make me laugh—I love you guys.

A big high-five to the many writers out there in cyber-space. Many of you I have yet to meet in person but your kind comments, encouraging words of support and your amazing talent are second to none. Thumbs up to the staff and students of Shawnigan Lake School; your interest and support means a lot.

A big thank you is in order for Ron, Veronica, Maria, and the talented team at Ronsdale Press. I have learned so very much from all of you, and your patience, guidance and encouragement are appreciated more than you know.

My biggest thank you goes to Richard, who always joins me on the couch for early-morning brainstorming sessions (whether he wants to or not). I appreciate your sharp wit and common sense, not to mention your superb coffee-making skills. I could not do any of this without you.

Chapter One

❧

HANNAH

THE FIRST THOUGHT I have when I wake up on Saturday is that school is almost over. And that means bare feet, a part-time job at the Salish Sea Studio, no more homework, and —and drum roll, please—actual high school in September. Finally!

I lie in bed waiting to feel different, but all I really feel is hungry. Poos and Chuck are fast asleep in their usual furry feline heap on my comforter so I shove them a little with my foot.

"Guys! School is practically done! Grade nine in September!"

Poos opens one sleepy eye but doesn't understand the significance of my statement and goes right back to sleep.

"Thanks for your enthusiasm." I shrug, and throw off my duvet. I walk over to my full-length mirror on the wall near the window and take a good look. Same old Hannah Rae Anderson. Same nutso hair. Same freckles. Same bony knees. I guess I'm taller than I was at the beginning of the year, but other than the new zit on my chin, there haven't been any miraculous transformations during the night.

There is a sudden commotion at my window. Both cats spring into the air and take off down my spiral staircase at warp speed. I smile. There's only one thing that would make them react that way first thing in the morning. Jack.

Sure enough, Jack is perched on the corner of the planter box outside my window, his legs hidden in a tangle of pink and white sweet pea blooms. He looks at me quizzically and moves his head up and down repeatedly like one of those hokey bobble-head animals people put on the dashboards of their cars.

"What are you so fired up about?" I ask him. The last few times he's visited he's been like this, kind of jumpy and hyper. When he tries unsuccessfully to squawk, I notice that he's carrying something in his beak.

"Oh, I get it. You've brought me another present?" I hesitate, because the last "gift" he brought me was half an old cigar. Totally disgusting.

Jack hops straight into the centre of the planter box and drops something into the flowers. I roll my eyes, stretch out my hand and feel around in the dirt for his present. I find it almost immediately, and hold it up between my face and Jack's beady black eyes.

"A beer cap? You've brought me a beer cap?" I turn it over in my hand. Big Mountain Lager. It's a popular beer on Vancouver Island but not exactly a collector's item. "You're losing your touch, buddy. I thought ravens were supposed to like jewelry and coins and stuff!" I reach up to touch the sliver of abalone that hangs around my neck. It's been there for two years now—the first thing Jack ever brought me. I've never taken it off. Not even once.

But Jack just caws in my face, flaps his blue-black wings, and takes off for the bay before I can say another word. I crane my head out the window and push aside the sweet peas but by the time I have a clear view, he's nothing but a black speck perched on the mast of the *Orca I*—an old abandoned tuna boat that's been rusting in the bay for years. Why Jack wants to hang out on that heap is a mystery to me, but he's been out there a lot lately. Jack isn't your average run-of-the-mill raven. Not by a long shot.

I put the Big Mountain beer cap up on the shelf next to the cigar butt. I should probably just throw them both away, but disgusting or not, a gift is a gift.

My cell phone buzzes from my nightstand and makes me jump. I'm still not used to having one. It was a middle-school graduation present from Aunt Maddie, much to my dad's despair.

"A cell phone, Madds?" he'd argued.

"She's a teenager, David!" Aunt Maddie had explained. "She'll be in high school soon. She needs a phone."

(Did I mention how much I love Aunt Maddie?)

Crossing to the phone now, I slide it open to reveal a text from Max: Hey! Want to meet me @ the Dog? I work at 10.

My stomach does a somersault, which I find surprising, and irritating as well. *Calm down. It's only Max.* But my stomach doesn't calm down. In fact, lately it performs complex gastric gymnastics whenever Max is around. I text him back: Sounds good. C U in 20.

I can't decide what to wear. It's June, so shorts and a t-shirt make sense but I'm just not in a shorts and t-shirt kind of mood. I mean, it's only breakfast, and its only Max, and it isn't like it's a date or anything, but still, a regular old t-shirt just doesn't feel right. So I put on my light green cotton skirt, a lilac tank top and my neon green flip flops, and then stand back to check myself out. I decide I look nice, but not in a stupid, dressed-up sort of way. My hair, however, is never easy, but because I only have ten minutes, I just twist it into submission and secure it in a lopsided messy bun with a barrette. It's just a temporary fix. I know it will look decent for about a minute at the most, and then half of my hair will find a way to escape for good. Story of my life.

"Well, well, well," Dad says when I come down the stairs. He's wearing his yellow "Marmite" shirt—it's one of his favourite foods, if you can believe it. Every sane person knows that Marmite is not fit for human consumption. The left side of his face is a roadmap of creases. "Look who's officially on summer vacation, and wearing a dress, no less!"

"It's not a dress!" I say defensively. "It's a skirt." And then to get my father's mind off my clothes, I say, "And school isn't over until Monday, so it's not officially summer vacay yet, Dad." It's true, although next week will be nothing but movies, junk food, and teachers checking their watches. "I'm just going to meet Max for a while."

Dad raises an eyebrow.

"I'll be back a little later. Okay?" I catch myself tapping my fingers on the side of the kitchen counter, and I consciously make myself stop. Still, I can't help noticing the clock. The minutes are ticking by at hyper-speed. I'm going to be late.

"Sure, honey," Dad says finally, reaching for his mug by the sink. He rinses it out and then places it beside the French press that he claims is the only way to make a decent cup of coffee. "Have fun."

"It's just breakfast," I say casually, but my voice gets drowned out by Dad's morning bean-grinding ritual. He presses the button in short bursts, instead of one long one, shaking the canister of beans between each grind. My dad is strange about coffee.

I raise my hand in a wave and he gives me a sleepy thumbs-up, then shuts off the grinder and shuffles over to give me one of his bone-crushing bear hugs.

"Your last summer, Hannah Banana, before real high

school!" he says, smelling like Italian dark roast.

"I know," I say, cringing. *Hannah Banana.* At fourteen, it's clearly time to retire that nickname.

"Grade nine in September." He shakes his head and stands back, crossing his arms across his chest. "Just quit growing up, will you? You make me feel decrepit."

"You *are* decrepit."

"Get outa here."

"I'm already gone." *And I'm already late.*

I know Max won't care. In fact, he probably won't even notice, but even so I decide to shave off a couple minutes by riding Mathilda. I lift my bike over the side rail of our houseboat and pedal up Dock 5, then hang a left until I reach the government wharf.

"Whoa, Hannah! Where's the fire?" Over on Dock 9, Riley Waters looks up from the *Tzinquaw*—his fish boat he anchors next to his houseboat—and wipes his forehead with his cap before placing it back on his head. His long white braid almost reaches to his waist. People say he looks like Willie Nelson.

"Hey, Riley." I wave. "No fire! Its just Mathilda. She's built for speed!"

Riley laughs, because this is *so* not true. My bike is ancient, older than me even, but it's still the best thing on two wheels in Cowichan Bay. Mom bought it when I was little, for twenty-five dollars from an Australian woman at a garage sale. Sure, it's clunky and only has five speeds, but it's a total work of art:

sky blue and white, with crazy cool aboriginal designs painted all over it. When Mom first brought it home, Dad built a contraption that attached over the front tire, a place for me to sit when Mom rode. He said I looked like a baby kangaroo up there, which was fitting, given the history of the bike. After Mom died, I kept the bike, as well as the carrier because it's good for hauling stuff around. Now that I'm fourteen, I guess I look a little strange cruising around on it, but there are lots of things about Dad and me and our life on our houseboat that people think are weird. Whatever. I'm okay with weird.

Chapter Two

꩜

ISABELLE (IZZY)

"WHY DON'T YOU GO visit Uncle James, Isabelle? He's one of the best artists around here. He could teach you some things."

I try to shut out Mom's voice while I concentrate on my sketchbook. Uncle James. Master carver. Right. Salmon and orcas, aka traditional Coast Salish art. Yawn. No thanks, Mom.

My mother and I are like oil and water. Isn't that the right expression? Describing two things that don't mix together very well? Yep, that would be us. It wasn't always this way, but ever since Dad left, Mom puts all her energy into "being busy" instead of "being motherly." She just doesn't *get* me. She doesn't even try. She hated my hair when I dyed it red, and she hated it even more when I cut it short. And it doesn't stop at my hair. She doesn't like my friends. My clothes. The books I read. She doesn't even like my artwork much.

"You know, you could draw something meaningful if you put your mind to it, Isabelle," she says. "You need to perfect the traditional designs first before you can alter them. You actually have some talent." *Actually*.

I don't have anything against tradition; some of those old-school designs are seriously cool. I just like to take them and put a contemporary twist on them. Because, come on ... same old, same old is boring, boring. "My drawings are meaningful to me," I argue, adding "and have you forgotten about my other half? My British half? Maybe I should go visit the Tate Gallery in London."

Mom doesn't answer me but she doesn't have to. Her expression says it all: that other half of me just doesn't exist.

On Saturday mornings, Mom runs a quilting class for a bunch of women who do more gossiping than sewing. Today she takes my kid sister, Amelia, with her so I'm free to catch a ride with Dylan to the town centre of Ganges. It's pretty much the only place to hang out on Salt Spring Island, and besides, I need cigarettes, a drawing pen and something to eat. There's never anything decent in our fridge these days.

"You want to go to Ruckle Park later?" Dylan asks once we're underway. "Everyone will be there. You know, an end-of-school kind of thing."

I roll down the window as we head toward town. "Maybe."

"Come on, Iz. You need to have some fun. You're so sour lately." Dylan smiles at me and pulls his ball cap farther down on his head. He's right. I haven't been much fun lately. It's just that Mom is so busy at the big house with band stuff and meetings and classes, and, as usual, it's me that has to keep it all together at home. I can't remember the last time she did laundry or cleaned the bathtub or bought Amelia some new socks. Just when exactly did I sign up for the job?

"It'll be worth it," Dylan singsongs as he fights static with the truck's radio. "We have *beeeer*."

When he drops me off in town, I buy smokes from Lawrence at the gas station. He's been selling them to me for a year now, which is great, except he charges me a buck more than they cost in the store, and that's annoying. Especially since I'm almost through all the money I've saved from baby-sitting the neighbourhood kids.

"I have to make a profit somehow, don't I?" Lawrence always laughs when I complain about the price tag. I reluctantly push the bills into his open palm.

"There's not a lot of money in selling smokes to kids, Iz," he says, tucking the cash into the chest pocket of his Carhartts.

"I'm fifteen." I frown. "And you're only nineteen, so don't go all preachy on me."

I make an unsuccessful grab for the pack of smokes but he's quicker than I am and raises his arm high above his head. I don't even try because Lawrence has got to be 6'4" and I'm only 5'2". Jumping for them would be a waste of time.

"Come on, Lawrence," I plead. "I paid for them." I want to turn and walk away, but I want the cigarettes more.

"You should quit."

"Yeah?" I say angrily. "So should you. You smoke, too."

"We're not talking about me." He smiles. He is clearly enjoying the game.

"Lawrence? Just give me the smokes." I hold out my hand and give him my best icy stare. The one that Mom says could jump-start another ice age.

He snorts and flicks the pack of cigarettes into the air with a flourish. I lunge to catch them, but they bounce off my thumb and land in an oily puddle a few feet away from where we're standing. I pick them up and shake off the greasy water. It's so humiliating.

Lawrence laughs and swaggers back into the station. When he raises his hand in a wave, he doesn't look back.

I cross the road to the drugstore. I can't wait until I'm old enough to buy smokes from here, and don't have to deal with that idiot anymore. I buy the pen, and a big bag of BBQ peanuts since I'm starving. There is nothing at home except some weird clam-and-dandelion-root thing Mom made from a new cookbook, *Coast Salish Cooking: Welcome to the Warmland*. Hasn't she ever heard of good old *Betty Crocker*? Thanks to her experimental cuisine, I'm forced to live on packets of Mr. Noodle and trail mix. I don't blame Dad for taking off. It's not like Mom ever made food that he liked. I don't remember any traditional fish and chips for him. Maybe that's why he left. Maybe he went straight back to England. He could be enjoying a nice scone and jam right now. I hear British people are stoked on afternoon tea. I wonder if he even remembers me, or if he even knows about Amelia? Mom was barely showing when he left. I wrote to him a lot in the beginning. Real letters. I sent them to his brother for almost three years but I never got an answer back. So I stopped.

I sit on the edge of the fence bordering Sam McMaster's apple orchard and eat the peanuts, which are a little stale. A minute later two sour-looking old women walk by on the side of the road and give me a withering look. *What's their problem?*

"Heavens! You wouldn't see kids looking like that in my day," one of them says as they pass. They both nod self-righteously, like they know everything and I know nothing.

I light a cigarette, and watch the old biddies until they disappear around a corner.

Good riddance.

Chapter Three

❦

HANNAH

I SPOT MAX OUTSIDE the door of the Salty Dog Café, leaning against the giant carved dog with the painted yellow rain slicker.

"Hey, Hannah!" he calls as I jump off my bike. He's wearing baggy cargo shorts, a turquoise t-shirt, and his favourite DC baseball cap that's sitting sideways on his head. He sure isn't the beanpole that he used to be. He has grown muscles. My stomach starts flipping around again. And again, it's irritating!

"Hey, Max." I lean my bike against the wrought-iron fence, suddenly conscious of my bony knees, and how my skirt seems way shorter now than it did when I put it on. Why didn't I just wear my board shorts, like I always do? Wearing a skirt on a bike is never a good idea. Everyone knows that. What was I thinking? Clearly, I wasn't.

"You look nice," Max says. He looks surprised and I feel my face grow warm. Do I normally look awful?

"Oh. Thanks. I guess." (*Dumb. Dumb. Dumb!*)

"So, you want to get a bagel or something? I don't have to work till ten."

I look at the crowd of people at the door waiting for tables.

"Or," I say, "we could just go for a walk or something."

"I was hoping you'd say that," Max says, smiling. "Besides, Nell gave me banana muffins on the way here. She said they were the wrong shape to sell."

I return the smile. Banana muffins from the Toad in the Hole bakery sounds like a pretty good breakfast to me, misshapen or not.

❧

"Where does that trail go?" I ask when we're off the main road and into the forest that butts up against Whitetail Farm. The morning sunlight filters through the Douglas firs and spills onto the sword ferns growing near the base of their trunks. Several quail, disturbed by our arrival, run single-file across the ground in front of us to disappear into the underbrush.

"Look at that," Max says, pointing to a crudely painted

piece of wood nailed to a tree near the opening. The word "Asparagus" is barely legible on the sign, the "gus" almost completely faded away. Whitetail Farm used to grow organic veggies. Now it's mostly just grass.

I hear something behind me, and for the first time I notice that Jack is here. He flaps his wings and hops energetically past us as if he's late for a bus.

"Where'd he come from . . . and where's he going?" I ask.

"Ask *him*. He's your raven, not mine."

"He's not *my* rave—" I stop. There's no point trying to explain. Jack is often a mystery, even though we've been pretty much inseparable for two years. "Come on back, Jack," I say, without much enthusiasm. Jack goes where Jack wants to go, so I shrug and follow him onto the trail.

"We're on private property," Max calls after me. "This trail doesn't go anywhere and it ends up ahead."

I keep walking after the trail ends, because even nowhere is somewhere, and a little bushwhacking is good for the soul. The lot may be private, but it's been for sale forever. Besides, I can think of worse ways to spend an hour than hanging out in the cool shade of the woods with Max Miller (who grew muscles).

I'm still thinking about this, when Max catches up.

"What?"

"Check that out." He points to something partially hidden behind a stand of bigleaf maples. "Looks like some moron dumped their garbage."

Sure enough, when we push back the foliage to investigate, we find six or seven garbage bags heaped any-which-way in the brush. Three are full of old potting soil that spills out through numerous rips in the bags, and a snaky mess of fried extension cords fills up another. A few more are full of beer cans and cigarette butts and there is a haphazard tower of plastic seedling flats sitting a few feet away, along with some empty boxes of "Fast-Gro" fertilizer. Jack hops over the pile and begins stabbing at the one of the bags with his beak.

Max picks up one of the plastic flats, turns it over, and shakes out a mixture of dried soil and seeds onto the ground. "I thought gardeners were ecologically minded."

"I have a feeling whoever dumped this stuff isn't growing petunias." I reach over to pick up two soggy business cards from one of the flats. One says, "Gary's Hydroponics—That's the Way We Grow," and the other, "Poseidon Salvage Inc." Both have random scribbles on the back, written in green ballpoint pen.

A few feet away, a twig snaps, and Max and I freeze. Another twig breaks, this one closer, and then another, and I stuff the cards into my pocket and grab hold of Max's hand. I don't even care that my palms are sweaty and cold with fear.

A familiar shaggy shape emerges from the bush, nose to the ground, wagging his comical stump of a tail. It's Quincy, Nell's dog: part Labrador, part Airedale, and part garbage can.

I drop to my knees and scratch his ears until he gives a little excited "woof." It's not the first time Quincy has escaped

Nell and the confines of the Toad in the Hole bakery to follow us.

"Come on, Han," Max says. "I guess we'd better head back. I have to work soon, anyway."

Quincy leads the way back to Cow Bay village, but Jack doesn't seem to want to leave. He keeps squawking and carrying on, hopping around beside the garbage pile. Crazy bird! We ignore him, and step around the clumps of Oregon grape and ferns, feeling the sun on our shoulders as the trees begin to thin out.

"Hey," Max says stopping. "I almost forgot. I have something for you."

"You do?"

"Yeah, I found it a few days ago and I saved it for you." He digs around in his pocket and then gestures for me to open my palm.

"It's nothing gross, right?" I've played this game before. Max can't always be trusted.

"Just open your hand flat," he says, rolling his eyes.

So I do, and he puts something into it—a box of matches.

"Um . . . " I start.

"Look inside."

And inside, is a perfectly shaped four-leaf clover. It must have taken him forever to find one. It's awesome, the most thoughtful gift in the world.

Last Christmas we exchanged gifts, but they were the jokey kind. I gave him a giant box of Fruit Loops because he is addicted to bad-for-you cereals, and he gave me one of those motion-sensored singing fish that he found at Trader John's Junk & Jewels up the road. It was missing an eye and had part of its fin torn away, but it was pretty funny, especially when we stuck it up above the door of Joe's Bait 'n' Tackle before they opened in the new year. Every time someone approached the shop, the fish began to sing out a super cheesy rendition of "Don't Worry. Be Happy." But this is no joke gift. I feel completely awkward and completely amazing all at the same time.

"Where did you find it?" I say, my voice smaller than I mean it to be.

"Near the estuary. I know you're superstitious and stuff so I figured you'd be stoked to have it. Consider it . . . I dunno . . . a graduation present or something. A lucky talisman for your future."

I carefully place it back inside the box, desperately trying to think of the right thing to say.

"Come on," Max says, breaking the awkward silence. "Let's go get a smoothie or something. I'm so down for a Mango Madness."

We part company with Quincy at the Toad, and then walk across the parking lot toward Udderly Delicious.

Max yanks me out of the way as a red pick-up truck backs out of a space, almost running me over.

"Whoa! Watch your step, honey!" The driver of the truck leans out the window and smooths down one side of his Fu

Manchu mustache. He's wearing a dirty red ball cap and a greasy smile. I frown at him. *Ever heard of a rearview mirror?*

A skinny man with blond hair and wearing a tight white t-shirt appears from around the back of Beckett's hardware store, pushing a cart filled with sacks of "Rural Roots Organic Potting Soil" and a big box of "Fast-Gro" fertilizer. He's got a tattoo of a grizzly bear on one forearm, and the name "Wake & Bake" inked up the other. Max and I watch as the two men heave the bags into the bed of the truck. I notice the two stickers on the back bumper: "Pacific Wind Boat Sales," and "Log it. Burn it. Pave it." *Nice.*

"Frikkin' expensive, this stuff," the skinny guy says when the cart is empty. He leans over to retie a shoelace. "Better be worth it."

"Oh, it'll be worth it," the guy with the red ball cap says. "Prime soil equals prime plants. It's a no-brainer."

"Hah! Listen to you. You're a regular Martha Stewart." The skinny guy flicks the ash from his cigarette onto his shoe and laughs, but the laugh quickly becomes a cough.

"Smokin' too much, Buzz?"

"Occupational hazard. Not to mention I—"

The skinny guy, Buzz, stops talking and looks straight at me and Max as though he's noticing us for the first time. He gives me a wink, and then says to his partner, "Come on, Kelso. It's almost beer o'clock. Let's get back to the . . . *garden.* Ray will be gracing us with his presence a little later, remember?"

The two of them bust up laughing, and a moment later the red 4x4 speeds up the road, the bass from its stereo still thumping after the truck has disappeared from sight.

"Never seen those guys before," Max says after they've gone.

"Me neither, but did you notice the box of fertilizer in the cart? It was the same kind we saw in the woods."

"Yeah, dopes buying "potting" soil. Get it?" says Max.

I groan. "Oh, ha, ha. You're so punny!"

We get our smoothies and sit at a picnic table outside, and talk about summer: my dad's upcoming vacation to Spain for book research, and the weird presents that Jack has been giving me lately.

"Maybe he's trying to tell you something?" Max suggests when we talk about the latest gift, the beer cap.

"What? That I should start smoking cigars and drinking Big Mountain beer?"

"I didn't say it had to make sense. That bird is kind of a head case."

"No, he isn't," I say, defending Jack. "He's highly intelligent."

Max looks at me dubiously, and then notices the time. "Whoa. It's almost ten. Better get to the Dog or Art will fire me for sure."

"Yeah, you don't want to succumb to the wrath of Art Lawson!" I say this in my best low-budget, horror-movie voice.

When we reach the restaurant, Max punches me on the shoulder. "Later, Anderson."

"Later. And thanks again, Miller. You know, for the clover." I touch the box, safe and sound in my pocket.

"Hope it brings you good luck." He smiles and reaches over to tug on a strand of my hair escaping from the barrette. "Your hair is ridiculous," he laughs, "but in a good way."

My stomach performs an energetic cartwheel, and I impulsively give him a hug, which I immediately regret. Guys get weird when you hug them, and Max is no exception. He turns red, backs up, and bumps straight into the door behind him.

"Uh. Okay. See you later, Hannah." He waves at me, even though I'm standing only inches away from him, and then quickly disappears inside the restaurant as though his feet are on fire.

Chapter Four

❦

IZZY

ALTHOUGH SALT SPRING Island is pretty much Nowheres-ville, Ruckle Park is nice. I come here a lot, usually to draw. Most of the time I just doodle, but occasionally I'll sit on the point and sketch the gnarled arbutus trees and bigleaf maples that grow close to the shoreline. But this afternoon I am content just to be with my friends and sit in the sun.

"Want another beer, Izzy?" Dylan interrupts my day-dreaming and hands me a can.

"Thanks." I set it down on the grass, stretch out on my back and close my eyes. The warmth of the sun on my face makes me sleepy. I sigh. How great would it be if I could just stay like this forever? With my eyes closed to the rest of the world, hearing nothing but the gulls crying out just past the rocks.

Most everyone is sitting just a little ways off: Dylan, Marika, Cody, and Jess. They're passing around a bottle—not beer, something stronger. As usual, Cody is making everyone laugh. He's good at that. He can mimic any accent under the sun, although his German one is my favourite. But this time it isn't Cody who holds my attention. It's Luke, a little farther off, stumbling around in the long grass with a cigarette hanging from his lips. He drinks too much. And lately, it's become worse.

"Luke!" I yell, shielding my eyes from the sun. "Get over here!"

He places a hand to steady himself on the side of the big green garbage can at the edge of the trail that leads to the beach. He raises his other hand in an enthusiastic wave. "Isabelle! Come on over here and dance with me, beautiful!"

"You're wasted!"

"Sure am! It's almost summer!"

"Luke, come over here before you hurt yourself," I say, but I've already shut my eyes and flopped back down on the grass. Luke marches to his own drummer. Always has. Besides, how much harm can he come to tripping around in the grass? It's not like he's near the water or the edge of a cliff.

Cody cranks up the volume on the ancient boom box he keeps in his car for such occasions, and soon the bass drowns out the seagulls. It's loud. Loud is good. Loud fills up my head so I can't think about anything other than the music.

Everyone is dancing. Jess and Dylan are clinging to each other as usual, but Marika is in her own world, swaying gracefully to the music with her arms outstretched on either side. Nobody can "hippie dance" like Marika.

I open my can of beer and walk over to join them on the bedrock where the grass ends. I drink the beer in just a few long swallows then toss it into the fast-growing pile of empties at the side of Dylan's blanket.

"Hey fools!" Luke yells from the grass. "Check this out!" He has a lighter in one hand and Marika's hairspray in the other.

"Dude!" Dylan yells. "Don't be an idiot."

I hear a WOOSH, and somebody—Marika, I think— screams. Everyone sobers up quickly as Luke's shirtsleeve catches fire. He rips the shirt from his body and throws the flaming fabric on the ground, hooting with laughter.

"The grass!" Jess yells. "Come on!"

As the flames lick the tinder-dry grass, Dylan sprints to the garbage can, retrieves the lid and smothers the fire. The area around it smokes, threatening to ignite, but we quickly stamp out the sparks, while the boom box continues to play an ear-splitting rap tune that, after all the drama, just seems too loud.

I reach over to shut it off, and that's when I see three cops approaching. They confront Dylan first, over by the garbage can, and then one of them signals for me to come over.

Great. Just great.

Chapter Five

❦

HANNAH

I UNLOCK MY BIKE, ignore my flip-floppy stomach, and turn around to smack right into Sabrina Webber. I back away from her like she's toxic waste (which, in my opinion, is not that far from the truth) and adjust my bike helmet. It suddenly feels abnormally large and ridiculous. Sabrina, of course, is dressed to kill, in a pair of skintight hipster jeans, a bright pink t-shirt that exposes a lot of her flat stomach, and a pair of fuchsia-coloured wedge sandals. In one hand she's holding a can of Diet Coke, and in the other, a pink leash. At the end of the pink leash is a small fluffy dog that has managed to twist itself around her ankles.

"Oh!" Sabrina says with fake concern. "Are you okay, Hannah?"

"Yeah, sure," I lie. How could bumping into Sabrina Webber first thing on a Saturday morning be even remotely okay?

"I totally didn't even see you there. Good thing you have your crash helmet on," Sabrina giggles. She has one of those tinkly, girly laughs that make me feel like throwing up.

"It's a bike helmet," I say.

Sabrina looks over at Mathilda leaning against the iron railing. "Oh, no way! You're still riding that little blue bicycle. Honestly, it's so totally adorable. Like something a little kid would ride. That is just so funny! So *you*, right?"

I'm not laughing.

"So, were you just hanging with Max or something?" Sabrina says coyly, jutting her hip out to one side and staring at me with unblinking blue eyes.

"Uh," I stammer, just as Max himself comes through the door. He's holding a giant green garbage bag in each hand, and when he sees us, drops the bags as if they were full of stolen goods.

"Oh. Hey Rina," he says, looking at Sabrina's t-shirt.

Rina?

"Hey, Max," Sabrina says in a voice that's higher than it was before. *Gag me.*

Max flushes, and bends down to scratch the thing at the end of the pink leash. "Cute dog. Isn't he a Pomeranian or something, or maybe a Shih Tzu? I didn't know you had a dog."

And I didn't know Max had a babbling problem.

Sabrina is beaming from behind her mascara-laden lashes and flashes a pink-frosted smile. She kneels down beside Max, and I feel completely invisible, except for my helmet, that is. It feels larger than ever, but I won't take it off on principle.

"Her name is Tiffany. Tiffy, for short. I got her three weeks ago. Mom is sort of choked about her, but she was a present from Daddy so she can't do a thing about it. Isn't she just capital 'C' cute?"

"Sure is," Max says, apparently the biggest foo-foo-stupid-dog-name dog appreciator in the world. "Check her out, Hannah." He has a big, stupid grin on his face.

"Oh," I say, maintaining my upright position next to my *adorable* bike. "Sure. Yeah. Cute, she is." The dog looks up at me with red and bulbous eyes that leave me wondering if it has a thyroid condition. It also has a prominent under bite. "Cute" is not the first word that comes to mind.

I drop my backpack into the carrier and push Mathilda away from the railing. "I have to go. I'll see you guys, later." I avoid looking at either of them, but not before I notice that Max has put on sunglasses. Aviators. When did he get those? Sabrina is practically leaning on him, the thyroid-challenged "Tiffy" neatly tucked under one of her already-tanned arms.

"Oh, sure thing, Hannah," she says cheerfully. "Got somewhere special to go?"

"Not really," I say under my breath. I place my foot on my bike pedal but when I make a clumsy effort to pedal away, my foot slips off and I bash my shin on the crank arm.

"Really?" Sabrina calls after me. "No travel plans this summer? No Sasquatches to stalk or caves to explore or anything?"

Mathilda wobbles and I lurch to the right, dropping my foot to the pavement just in time to prevent an awkward fall.

"Pardon me?"

"Oh, nothing. I just figured that after your little 'adventure' two years ago, you might have been bitten by the travel bug," Sabrina says, rolling her eyes at Max, who looks awkwardly at the ground.

"Uh. No." I try my hardest to remain calm. "No travel plans this summer."

"Well," Sabrina says, "you'd better stay out of the woods then. Isn't that right, Max?"

Max turns redder and picks up both of the garbage bags again, even though he looks like he doesn't know what he's supposed to do with them. "Woods? Oh. I guess. Sure. The woods can be freaky. Bears and cougars and stuff. Right. Okay. I better go dump this compost, I guess."

"I'll keep you company, Max. And . . . I guess I'll see you Monday, Hannah."

The two of them walk off quickly toward the back of the restaurant, and as I pedal out to the main road, I hear Sabrina's nauseating giggle pretty much above all else. I pedal faster and faster, passing by all the stores in a blur, until I reach the top of the hill past the village. I lay my bike down in the shade of a chestnut tree, and catch my breath. My chest feels tight and my mouth is dry. I wish I'd brought water with me, but I hadn't planned on breaking any speed records in a stupid too-short green skirt this morning.

I stand there like the idiot I am, staring vacantly out to the sea, trying to process the one-sided conversation I've just had with Sabrina.

She knows! She knows about two summers ago! About the cave. About travelling back in time. About all the stuff that happened after I found the spindle whorl. She knows about the Thumquas and Yisella and . . . *everything*!

Max was the only person I told about all that stuff, because it was Max who found me back at the cave when I "came back." I told him everything! I told him about the village in Cowichan Bay. The way it was all those years ago. I told him about Yisella, the girl I'd dreamed about and finally met there. I told him how her mother had died from smallpox and about the sailors off the HMS *Hecate* who chased us through the woods. And Jack. How Jack had started it all. How he'd gone back in time with me.

"*Hannah!*"

I turn to see Max running up the hill, his ball cap clutched in his left hand. No. Way. No way can I talk to him right now! I get back on Mathilda and begin to pedal away from him.

"Hannah! STOP! Stop!"

"GO AWAY!"

"Come on! I need to talk to you!"

So I stop. Max stands a few feet in front of me, trying to

catch his breath. His damp shirt is stuck to his chest and his face is bronzed and shiny.

"How could you do that?" I hiss through clenched teeth.

"Do what?"

"You *told* her!" I say. "You told her everything!"

"No," Max says, "I didn't! I never said a word."

"LIAR!" I yell. Does he think I'm stupid? My hands grip my handlebars tighter and my face grows hotter. I want the ground to open up and swallow me whole. No! I want the ground to open up and swallow *Max* whole!

"Hannah, I never—"

"You can't just stand there and deny it!" I force back tears. I can't believe this. He may as well have punched me in the stomach, because that's what it feels like. Like the wind has been knocked out of me. Like I'm suddenly made of paper and might just curl up and blow away. "You were the only person I told! I trusted you!"

"Look! Just listen! I didn't tell Sabrina anything! You think I actually want people to know what a psycho you were back then?"

I forget how to breathe. I stand there, not moving, staring at this person that I thought was my best friend. Someone who now seems like a complete stranger.

"Hannah." Max steps forward, but I'm silent. I can't move. I just stand there, holding onto my bike, blinking. "Look. I'm sorry. I shouldn't have said that. That's not what I mean at all."

"Forget it," I say, when I'm finally able to speak, so upset that my cheeks are now wet. I swipe at them angrily and turn to push my bike off the verge but Max takes hold of my arm.

"Will you just chill for a second, Hannah? I get it, okay? Your mom died. You were only ten. I've read about it. Post-traumatic stress syndrome. All kinds of crazy stuff can happen to people who have gone through what you went through. People can imagine all sorts of—"

"Imagine?"

"Yeah, people can hallucinate, and imagine that dreams are real and stuff. They sometimes get confused. It doesn't mean you're crazy. It's just the way some people cope with stress."

I look at him hard and he stares right back at me. Neither one of us says anything for what seems like a long time, but eventually it's me who breaks the silence. "Aren't you supposed to be working?"

Max shrugs. "It's all good. Don't worry about it."

"I'm not. And I have to go."

"No," he says. "Don't. You're still mad."

Before he can stop me, I'm on my bike and flying back down the hill. I don't bother looking behind me, and I don't listen when Max yells my name. I don't stop pedalling until I'm back at the government wharf's gate. I undo the latch, push Mathilda through, and let the gate slam shut behind me.

A minute later I'm on the deck of our houseboat, wiping furiously at my cheeks, wondering how I'm going to put on a happy face for the rest of the day. If this is what the summer has in store for me, I am so not impressed.

❦

"Hannah, you've barely touched your cheesecake!" Aunt Maddie says, poking me in the ribs with her finger.

I give her a brave smile and pick up my fork. Ever since this morning, I've sort of lost my appetite, but Dad was so excited about bringing me here, I couldn't bail.

Figaro's Bistro is our favourite place to eat in the whole of Victoria, but even so, I just can't get my mind off what happened earlier. I still can't believe Max could betray me like that.

Dad leans across the funky hand-painted table and studies my face. "Who are you and what have you done with my daughter?"

Under normal circumstances, dessert and I are the best of friends, but tonight I manage only a couple of bites. As usual, Figaro's is busy, and even though we get a nice table near a window, the hand-painted tablecloths and colourful artwork on the deep burnt sienna walls fail to lift my spirits. But I take another bite of my "school's-almost-over" raspberry, choco-late-marbled cheesecake and force a smile, for Dad and my aunt's benefit.

"Oh, I'm just savouring it," I say.

"Well, don't savour it for too much longer, or I'm going to savour it for you," Aunt Maddie says, and then babbles on in her usual style, about how she's learning Mandarin, and how her neighbour's labradoodle had to have surgery to remove a pine cone from its stomach, and how she's stressing about Grandma's leaky septic field in Parksville. Sometimes it gets irritating listening to her talk, but tonight I'm grateful for the noise. I push the cheesecake around on my plate and try not to think about Max or Sabrina, or two summers ago.

I'm not very successful. Why is it that the thing you don't want to think about ends up consuming every square inch of your brain? I reach up to touch the abalone shell around my neck, and right away I'm back in Tl'ulpalus. I'm not crazy now and I wasn't crazy then. I was there! I have my necklace to prove it, and I have Poos as well. Living, breathing, furry feline proof. He came back with me. Those moments are still crystal clear in my mind. I can see Yisella's face. I can hear the drums of her village. I can smell wood smoke and taste the dried salmon and still see those giant cedar trees standing like silent soldiers deep in the forest.

"Isn't that right, Han?" Dad asks, and I snap back to reality.

"Sorry. What did you say?"

"I was just saying . . . how great it will be when they move that rust bucket of a ship out of the bay. You were talking about it the other day. The *Orca I*. Remember?"

I chase a bit of chocolate drizzle around the plate with my finger. "Oh. Yeah. Riley says it's scaring the fish away."

"Really?" Aunt Maddie asks.

"Apparently," I say. "He says it's an environmental disaster area. Ben said the same thing."

"Ben and Riley are a couple of old coots," Dad says, shaking his head. He looks into his coffee cup, and when he sees that it's empty, he begins scanning the restaurant for our waitress, a look of desperation on his face. Dad can't seem to go five minutes without a fresh cup. He probably needs an intervention.

"Maybe," I tell him, even though Ben and Riley are two of our favourite people on the docks, "but they know about fish and boats."

"True," Dad agrees. "Heard someone got the salvage rights to it, though. Thirty-five metres of rust and barnacles."

"So much drama, lately," Aunt Maddies says. "Derelict boats. Animal poaching. Grow-ops. The Cowichan Valley used to be so quiet and peaceful."

"Animal poaching?" I perk up. Mr. Rodman, our social studies teacher, was talking about Roosevelt elk awhile ago. About how you can only hunt them in October, and even then you have to buy a "tag" that says you're allowed. They only sell a few of them because the number of elk are dwindling. Mr. Rodman said there was a pit-lamping incident up in Youbou recently. That's when trucks come in from all angles and shine their high beams on an unsuspecting herd. It totally stuns them so it makes it easy for hunters to shoot them from their trucks, even the babies—the calves. It makes me feel sick just thinking about it.

"It's sickening," Aunt Maddie says. "A rash of animal remains turned up lately—eagles, and abalone from up past Bamfield, and now elk remains. What's wrong with people?"

"Power of the almighty dollar," Dad says. "Some folks will do anything for money."

⁂

It's growing dark by the time our old Jeep Wagoneer crawls back up the Malahat toward home. It was a nice dinner, but I don't really want to be a part of the conversation between Dad and Aunt Maddie. Sitting in the back seat suits me just fine.

I lean my head back on the seat and gaze out the half-open window. The water of Finlayson Arm is black and still, and up above, the first few stars begin to appear. It's a perfect summer evening, the kind that usually leaves me feeling content and peaceful. But I don't feel that way tonight.

I reach into the pocket of my jeans and pull out my cell phone to check for messages. Nothing. I practically throw it down on the seat beside me, vowing not to check it until tomorrow, but of course I spend the rest of the drive listening for the familiar "ping" of an incoming text. All I hear for the rest of the ride home is Aunt Maddie's constant chatter, and some old Van Morrison on the Jeep's CD player. "Tupelo Honey."

But later on, when I'm lying in bed, my depression is replaced with impatience. I tell myself to suck it up. If Max wants to be a jerk, then Max can be a jerk. I know it happened, and no one will ever be able to take that summer back in time away from me. Not ever.

Hours later, there is a commotion outside my window again, and just as before, Poos and Chuck are not happy about the rude awakening. Sure enough, when I get up to investigate I discover Jack back in the window box, but this time he isn't content just hopping about in the sweet peas. This time, he adds some irritating beak-rapping against the glass, even though the window is mostly open.

Jack has never visited this late before.

"Jack! What are you doing?"

I open the window a little wider, only to have him drop something straight into the palm of my hand, and I can tell right away that it's no beer cap. I switch on the lamp beside my bed and inspect my palm; Jack becomes strangely still and quiet in the planter box. It's a claw. A bear claw. I know this because Mr. Sullivan from the museum had a bunch in his office when we first showed him the spindle whorl two summers ago.

"Where did you get this?" I ask Jack. He cackles quietly and hops from one foot to the other, as is his habit, and then without so much as a how-do-you-do, he launches himself and heads toward the water. I put the claw up on the shelf beside the other "treasures" from Jack, and then look out the window to see where he's gone. It's dark. There are a couple of lit windows in the cottages on the shore, but all the boats in the harbour aren't much more than dark shapes on top of the even darker water. Except for one. I strain my eyes in the night, trying to focus them on a particular boat that sits farther out from the rest. The *Orca I*. I can't tell for sure but I think I see a dull glow coming from one of the dirty windows in the hull. Really? Someone is actually out there? I blink a couple of times, straining to see more, but moments later I can't be sure if it's just my eyes playing tricks on me. The light seems to have disappeared. It's impossible to tell whether Jack is on the boat, but he's out on the water somewhere.

Sleep is impossible. Now I'm thinking not only about Max and Sabrina, but also about Jack and cigar butts, beer caps, and bear claws.

Chapter Six

❧

IZZY

I SLAM THE KITCHEN door and walk out to the dusty road in front of my house. It's the first time I've gone outside since the whole Ruckle Park fiasco. I stare at the field across the road and then to the ocean beyond where the evening sun is lighting up the water.

An old blue pickup crests the hill and then slows to a stop in front of me. Dylan. He leans out the window and grins at me. "Where you been?"

"Around."

"Want to go hang out at Lost Lake?"

"Can't," I tell him, unable to meet his eyes.

"Ah, sure you can. Why not?"

"You didn't hear what happened? Mom is getting rid of me for the summer." I shoot him an icy look, and then immediately regret it. It isn't Dylan's fault my life sucks.

"Right," he says, staring at me intently. "Jess told me. That sucks, Iz." He leans a little farther out the window. "And Luke is a complete dumb ass. If he hadn't pulled that stunt with the hairspray, the cops—"

"It doesn't matter," I say, kicking at a stone on the side of the road. "At least he wasn't really hurt."

This isn't Luke's fault, but the cops calling Mom was the last straw, the final excuse she needed to send me packing. "Your friends aren't good for you, Isabelle," she'd said. "I'm worried about you, drinking beer and setting fires. What's next?"

"Are you leaving tonight?" Dylan asks.

"No."

"When, then?"

"Soon. When school's done."

He cuts the motor and the car's engine spits, hiccups, and then dies. "Well, you're going to miss some awesome parties."

I shrug and look out to the middle of the road again, focusing on three crows that are pecking at what looks like the remains of a raccoon.

Dylan starts up the truck. "Come on. Come to the lake. No beer this time, but Cody has some good weed. You could use a toke or two."

"Thanks, but I'm grounded," I say. I've never really been

into the whole pot thing anyway, even though my friends are.

"Well, maybe we'll come visit you this summer, okay? Cow Bay isn't far from here."

"Sure." Maybe my friends will visit. Maybe they won't. My father said the same thing on his way out the door all those years back. "Don't be sad, Iz. I'll come visit soon." People are always making promises they don't keep.

I don't watch the truck drive away. If I do, I'll just imagine all of us—Dylan, Cody, Marika, Jess, and Luke—sitting in the back of Dylan's pickup, listening to music down at the beach. Instead, I turn around and walk slowly back to our house.

I sit on the front step, next to the cracked terra cotta pot of wilting yellow chrysanthemums, and begin to pull off the dried, curled leaves. A moment later, my little sister sits down beside me.

"Izzy?" Amelia says, sitting as close to me as space will allow.

"Yeah?"

"Can I come with you? To Cowichan Bay? I could help look after you."

I look down at my sister's large dark eyes and earnest expression and can't help smiling. She's got to be the sweetest kid on the planet. Not an evil bone in her body. It's hard to believe that we share the same DNA. "I don't need looking after, Amelia."

"Yes, you do. Least that's what everyone says. They say that's why you're going to stay with Ramona. So you won't get into any more trouble."

"That's what they're saying, huh?"

"Uh-huh. They say you have to learn to follow rules. Then you'll remember how to be good again." Amelia nods her head as though she truly believes this.

"Am I that bad, Meely?"

"No. I think you're a good big sister."

"Thanks."

"Mom says you don't like it when people tell you what to do, so that means you're stubborn."

I chuckle. "You like it when people tell you what to do, Amelia? Do you like it when they make you sit at the kitchen table until you finish your broccoli?"

Amelia makes a face. "I hate broccoli."

"Well, you see? We're not so different, then."

"Do you hate broccoli too?"

"Can't stand it." I frown, even though I don't mind it.

The front door opens and Mom comes out. I don't look up at her but out of the corner of my eye I can see she's got her hair in a ponytail, tied with a brightly woven piece of fabric—probably one of Ramona's creations. Bright and cheery, just like Ramona.

"Dinner's ready, girls," she says in a quieter than normal voice.

"Not hungry," I say back.

"Is it broccoli?" Amelia asks, looking worried.

"No. It's macaroni and cheese. Izzy's favourite," Mom says proudly. It's the first meal she's prepared in weeks that doesn't involve some overcooked indigenous root vegetable.

"YUM!" Amelia is up off the stoop and into the house in a

flash. I remain sitting on the step. Mom sits down beside me, looking tired.

"Are you going to give me the silent treatment forever?" she asks.

"Maybe."

"Come on, Isabelle. You get to spend the whole summer in Cowichan Bay, with Ramona. You used to like Ramona. Come to think of it, you used to like a lot of things." She pats my hair down, trying to make it less spiky, then joins me in picking off dead chrysanthemum heads from the pot.

"How do you know what I like? Besides, Cowichan Bay is boring."

"Cowichan Bay is our real home, the home of our ancestors," Mom says proudly.

Fasten your seatbelt. Here we go.

"So why don't *you* go, then."

"Because I have to do the markets. And there's knitting to do. And of course there's the community garden at Fulford Harbour. I'll visit in a few weeks. I promise."

"Don't bother."

"Izzy..."

"No! I mean it. I hate you for this, Mom! All my friends are here and you're making me spend my whole summer knitting? You *know* that's not my thing! It's *your* thing. Why can't you just be proud of me the way I am?" I move away from her on the step, even though my arm ends up getting scratched in the spiky tangle of wild roses growing beside me.

"I am proud of you, Isabelle," Mom says, reaching out to

touch my cheek, but I push her hand away. "You're capable of so much, honey. If you'd just stop being so angry all the time and give people a chance, you—"

"Don't act like everyone cares, Mom! No one does."

Mom looks confused, and a little hurt, and I wonder what it must be like inside her head. She's so naïve. It's not normal to be so positive all the time.

"It's true," I say. "A week from now everyone here will have forgotten me."

"You know? Your ancestors hear you when you say things like that, Isabelle. You'll shame them. You come from Cowichan Bay. You should be excited! In a way it'll be like going home."

"Mom?" I tilt my head back and close my eyes. "Please don't go all *Indian* on me again. You take all that stuff way too seriously. It's totally embarrassing." I reach forward to pick up a handful of pebbles from the base of the step, dropping them one by one into an empty milk bottle on the ground beside me.

Mom stands up, brushes off the backs of her legs, and crosses to the front door. "Your dinner is on the stove," she says as she leaves, without even looking at me.

But I'm just not hungry, not even for my mother's home-made macaroni and cheese, which is the only good "normal" food she can make.

I go inside anyway so I don't have to stare at the ocean anymore.

Chapter Seven

⁂

HANNAH

I ALTERNATE BETWEEN hating Max with the white-hot intensity of a thousand suns, and missing my total best friend of two years.

When we get back from Victoria, I lie awake for hours until I decide to go and sit at the end of our dock to watch the sun come up over Mt. Tzouhalem. That never gets old. I've done it millions of times.

I yank the grey blanket from the foot of my bed and roll it up under my arm. Poos and Chuck, who have resettled themselves after Jack's untimely visit, look irritated when I pull the blanket out from under them, and are forced to re-arrange themselves on top of my sweatshirt. They close their eyes and fall back to sleep right away, reaffirming my desire to come back as a cat in my next life. Cats can sleep eighteen hours straight if you let them. Sleep, tuna fish and chin scratches. Might be boring, but at least you wouldn't have to worry about your best friend betraying you.

Sneaking past Dad's room is no big deal. I can hear him snoring even before I'm down the stairs. He won't be up for hours.

Cowichan Bay at dawn is awesome. I never get tired of watching the marina come to life, and it's especially magical in the summertime. I know it won't be long before the smells of coffee and cinnamon and bacon will settle over the boats, and an hour after that, the tourists will start to appear along the main road, eager for the shops to open. But right now, at the end of the dock, it's quiet and dark—the way it always is just before the sun comes up. I don't see or hear anything except the water slapping against the barnacle-covered dock post beside me. All I can smell is the ocean and the slightly fishy, creosote odour that is always here.

Jack arrives a moment later, swooping down low over my head as he heads toward the fog out in the distance. I hope he has no more presents in mind for me today. But a few seconds later I think I see him settle on the mast of the abandoned *Orca I* as though he's waiting for something, or someone. Maybe I wasn't seeing things last night. Maybe Jack noticed the light in the boat's window as well?

And then, just as though someone has read my mind, a light *does* go on, in the same window as before. I jump up and rest a hand against the post beside me, leaning forward to see more clearly. But it's gone. Or is it? No! It's back. Dim, but definitely there. I scan the length of the boat, looking for any sign of life, but the *Orca I* is just a black shape in the distance, and Jack, a small black blob on top of her mast.

A motor starts up. It sounds like it's coming from near the *Orca I* but then again, sound does strange things when it's out on the water. It's hard to be sure.

A moment later I think I see something in the half-light that makes me wonder if I am hallucinating. Despite the low fog now rolling in, I see something move. I squint harder at the shape and pull my blanket right over my head with a shiver.

There it is again! A boat near the stern of the *Orca I*—at least I think it's a boat. It's so hard to focus and a second later the fog swallows up whatever is out there and the shape is gone.

Yet I can still hear it! The grumble of the motor is low and muffled, almost an idle, and I move my head from left to right, trying to locate its source. Then it stops just as suddenly as it began, and is replaced by a voice. A man's voice. He yells something, but in the moments that follow, everything is quiet.

Then through the fog, I see flashes of orange—a zodiac, or some kind of big inflatable tender that is definitely carrying two people. They head toward Skinner Bluff, and then around the point in the direction of Genoa Bay.

I watch as they enter another bank of fog, but when it dissipates, so do they. It's like someone flipped a switch! Were they ever there at all? Am I losing my mind? Maybe it's sleep deprivation. I've heard insomniacs can go crazy. Wait . . . I saw two people in a boat. Who *were* they? And what were they doing near the *Orca I*? And why were they doing it at 4:30 in the morning?

The fog continues to roll in, thicker now, and it isn't long before the *Orca I* has vanished along with everything else— all except for the top of her mast, where Jack sits, also watching.

"Hey!"

I nearly jump out of my skin! It's Ben, who, as usual, has appeared out of nowhere. Locals don't call him the "Nautical Ninja" for nothing. He shines his flashlight full in my face.

"Ben!" I screech. "Cut it out!"

"Hannah? That you? What in hell you doing down here at 4:32 in the morning?" He looks at his watch and then switches off the light and sits down beside me. He's dressed in his work pants, a red-plaid flannel shirt and his usual green down vest covered with tacky fishing lures. When he pulls out a pack of cigarettes from his pocket and knocks one into his hand, I'm pretty sure he's waiting for me to tell him why I'm out here.

Instead I say, "You should quit."

"And you should still be sleeping, not hanging around the docks in the dark."

"Whatever."

"Why so sour?"

"I'm not," I say flatly.

"Are too."

"Am not."

"Are too."

"Whatever," I say again.

"That your new favourite word?" He flicks open a silver lighter and lights his cigarette.

"Maybe."

"Come on, Han. Spill. What's up?" He takes a long draw from the cigarette and blows a stream of smoke out in front of him. I shift over a few inches, because while Ben is great, his cigarettes aren't.

"Do you ever see weird things out there on the water?" I ask him.

He laughs. "How much time do you have?"

"Really? Like what sort of things?"

"Been on boats my whole life. Seen some pretty crazy stuff out there."

"Like sea monsters?"

"Maybe," he says, scratching the stubble on his chin. "But I'm not the only one, you know. There are stories about these waters that go way back. Stories about Cow Bay, in fact." He takes another pull on his cigarette, and the end of it glows in the dark.

I consider telling him about the *Orca I* and the people in the boat and about Jack and the weird "presents" he's brought me, but decide against it. I can't handle anyone else thinking

I'm crazy, especially when I'm not convinced myself. Besides, Ben gets fired up easily, and Dad is always telling me not to encourage him with my stories.

"There's this one story about a sea monster here in Cow Bay," Ben says, scratching his chin. "A giant orca that hung out near the mouth of the river over there, causing trouble. People didn't know what to do. In the end, a giant Thunder-bird—*Tzinquaw*—swooped in to save the day. Picked up the orca and got rid of him for good."

"A Cowichan legend?" I ask.

"You know it," Ben says. "So many legends about orcas and eagles. Smart critters. After all, our friend Riley wouldn't name his boat after just *any* old bird."

"Do the Cowichan believe that every orca is trouble?"

"Nah, not trouble, just powerful—worthy of our respect—that kind of thing, except for that stink pot out there," Ben says, squinting out to the *Orca I*. "Now *that* orca is a lot like the one in the legend. Riley says its bad news."

"What makes him say that?" I stiffen, wondering if Riley has seen the same things I've been seeing lately.

"Just a feeling in his guts."

"That's it?" I snort.

"Don't laugh, Hannah. Riley's gut is always right."

Again I think about telling Ben about the tender, but before I can open my mouth he says, "You know, all my orca experiences have been good ones. Had one push my tender out of a rip current once. Saved my arse."

"Really?"

"Yup."

I smile when he says "arse." It's one of Max's favourite words, and it always makes me laugh because . . . well, what fourteen-year-old says "arse"?

Max. Why did I have to go and think about him?

"You ever have a best friend, Ben?"

"Well, sure," he says. "Sadie rates right up there."

"No, I mean a *real* best friend."

"I'd have to say Sadie is about as real as they come."

I sigh. Sadie is Ben's African Grey parrot, notorious for her colourful language and knack for stealing food off people's barbecues. And while Sadie and Ben are pals, I doubt they discuss complex matters of the heart. It just isn't the same. Besides, Ben is a sixty-one-year-old fisherman. What does he know about teenagers?

"Forget it," I say. "It doesn't matter. I'm fine."

"You sure about that?" Ben says. "You don't seem fine to me. Seems like maybe you should come up to the Toad and visit Nell with me while she bakes. Have a hot chocolate or something. Sweeten yourself up."

"Ew!" I say, still scowling. "I hate hot chocolate." But even I have to admit that I sound like a six-year-old brat.

"Suit yourself," he says, wincing as he gets up, putting weight on his bad hip. He hesitates for a minute, waiting for me to change my mind, and when I don't, he points his flashlight out at the water and turns it on and off in three short bursts, then again in three longer ones, then three short ones again.

"What are you doing? Trying to scare the fish?"

"It's an SOS." Ben chuckles. "I'm calling for help. Cranky teenage girls scare me." Then he shrugs and walks back up the dock toward the shore.

Three short bursts, then three longer ones, then three short ones again. Yeah, like people have got time to do *that* when their boat is sinking. I rearrange the blanket around my shoulders and frown out to the sea, feeling worse than ever. I shouldn't be rotten to Ben. I've known him since I was in diapers. Standing up, I take one last look across the bay. A pale pink finger of light hangs over Mt. Tzouhalem, and a couple of turkey vultures circle overhead, killing time before they can hitch a ride on the afternoon thermals.

The *Orca I* itself remains quiet and unchanged, the way it has looked ever since it was ditched out there three years ago. The only thing different these days is that Jack seems to have made it his home away from home.

Chapter Eight

IZZY

WHEN LUKE DROPS by to say goodbye, he's clearly had one too many beer. After he leaves, Mom goes ballistic. *"We have to get you away from those kids, Isabelle! They're a bad influence on you!"* So now, instead of doing nothing at school for the last couple of days of the year like a normal teenager, I'm stuck in our van, waiting for a boat to nowhere.

"It's not my fault the ferry is late," I say, staring at the glove compartment. It's going to be a long day.

"Oh, dear. Who knows how long we'll be stuck here," my mother says anxiously.

"Is it that big a deal?" I ask. What's her rush? Geez, I'm surprised she didn't handcuff me, too.

"I just hope we don't have to wait too long. How many cars does the ferry take? Do you remember? Do you think we'll get on, Iz? What if the car in front is the last one they let on. How frustrating will that be?" Mom is clearly flustered and wrings her hands together nervously on her lap. I can tell she's in one of *those* moods. The kind where she talks more than she breathes. I don't think I can take it. Not today.

We're in the overflow vehicle lineup at the Vesuvius/Crofton ferry, on our way to Vancouver Island, and a guy in the car ahead has his bare feet sticking out the back window and his radio blasting.

"I'm getting out for a while," I say. The thought of being imprisoned in a hot vehicle with my motor-mouth mom for an undetermined length of time is unbearable.

"You can get out if you want, but keep your eye on the van. I don't want to miss the boat because you've gone off drawing in the trees or something. And don't get into trouble!"

I'm already out of the van.

"Bring me a coffee?" she calls after me.

The ferry lot is full and the heat rising off the tarmac is intense, typical for August, but unusual for June. I run my hands through my hair. It feels sticky and gross—too much gel, but I'm thankful it's so short. I head for the public washroom beside Mother Nature's Kitchen—a stand that sells cookies made of birdseed as well as herbal teas—just to have a moment to myself.

When I open the door I'm relieved to find that it's empty. I don't want to make small talk with anyone, or put up with the disapproving stares I know I'll get when I light up the cigarette I've been dying to have for over an hour.

I find a cubicle, take out my cigarettes and matches from my bag, and light up. I lean back against the door, inhale deeply, and try to imagine a wide green field. A soft breeze. Yellow daisies. I read somewhere if you picture a peaceful scene, it can relax you. But it doesn't work for me. As soon as I see the field of daisies, I see my mother and her posse of wool-obsessed, basket-weaving Cowichan friends, stomping toward me, barking at me not to step on the native plants.

What kind of mother ships her kid off because of a little harmless partying at the beach? It wasn't my fault Luke got so wasted. And I only had a couple of beers. Why am I being punished? If Ramona had kept her nose out of our business, everything would have been fine.

I lean forward and flick the ash from my cigarette into the toilet. Ramona. *So* stoked about being half-Cowichan, unable to resist the chance to do her good deed of the year: *help a directionless First Nations youth rediscover her roots.* Blah blah blah. Broken record. Why doesn't Ramona have the same enthusiasm for her Scottish ancestry? Why isn't she out there making tartan shopping bags to carry a haggis in alongside her knitted Cowichan sweaters? What's with that?

"You'll love the bay," my grandfather had said. "It'll grow on you. And it will be good for you to get off Salt Spring, Izzy. See a little bit of the world!"

But what does he know? He's hardly been away from the Gulf Islands in all of his sixty-eight years. None of my family ever goes anywhere, unless of course, you count Dad, who could be . . . well, I guess he could be anywhere. Oh, and my cousin Alfred, but look where it got him; he's pretty much living on the streets on the east side of Vancouver with no fixed address. So much for seeing the world.

I smoke the cigarette down to the filter before I flush it away, and pop a breath mint, carried for just such an occasion. I push the door open but before I can exit, a woman comes in dragging a screaming toddler. The little girl is gasping, pulling at her mother's hand and trying to fling herself to the ground. Her face is almost purple.

"You know you have to go!" the woman yells at the little girl.

"I don't! I don't have to pee! I went already! Let. Me. Go!"

I frown. I'm sure the kid knows if she has to go to the bathroom or not. Why do adults think they always know what their kids need? As I leave, I shoot the angry mother an icy glare, which she returns.

I stop at Mother Nature's Kitchen and dutifully buy an organic black coffee for Mom and one of the less seedy-looking cookies for myself. When I get back to the van, Mom is shuffling through a bunch of leaflets on her lap. She brightens when she sees I remembered her coffee, and then flaps a brochure enthusiastically in front of my face. "Look, Izzy! There's a market in Cowichan Bay every weekend! Maybe your knitting will get better. Maybe you'll be as good as Ramona and sell your own stuff there along with hers! Make some real money for yourself!"

Here we go again. I don't answer. Instead, I look out the window and see a man in a yellow t-shirt walking a dog at the edge of the road. He stops and ties the dog—a hound with big soft ears—to a bike rack before wandering off towards the craft stands.

"I have a feeling you're going to get into the whole knitting thing, Izzy. Because remember, all the women in our family are all good at—"

I get out of the van and walk over to the dog. It begins to wag its tail furiously the closer I get, and there is a long string of drool hanging down from one side of its jowly mouth.

"Hey, buddy," I say, extending a hand. The hound sniffs at it and sits down, his wagging tail spraying gravel left and right on the ground behind him like a windshield wiper. I smile when he licks the side of my face with his big, raspy tongue.

"Uh-oh. Sorry about Boomer. He's usually shy. Normally gets kind of spooked by most people." The man has returned, a yogurt cone in his hand.

"I don't mind. I like dogs."

I give Boomer a final scratch behind his floppy ears and stand up. He looks at me with brown liquid eyes, so trusting and warm, and places a paw on my leg.

"Well, nice to meet you, too," I tell the dog, shaking the paw.

"That's weird," the dog's owner says, looking surprised. "He doesn't usually warm up to people so fast. Usually takes him a long time to make friends."

It doesn't seem weird to me at all.

Chapter Nine

BY EARLY EVENING, my eyes are all scratchy as if they've been rolled around in a tray of kitty litter and then stuck back into my head.

"Go to bed early, kid," Dad says to me. We're sitting on the deck sharing a bowl of microwave popcorn under the strand of chili-pepper lights that Aunt Maddie bought us because she said they were cheerful. "You look tired."

"That's a good idea," I say. I pass the bowl of popcorn back and stand up, stretching my arms high over my head while I stare like a zombie at nothing in particular.

"You okay, Han?" he says. "You don't seem yourself."

I brace myself for one of his awkward, "concerned father"

talks. It's not that I don't appreciate his attention, but he never really knows what to say at times like these, and I end up having to lead the conversation, which is sometimes more work than not talking at all. I came to the conclusion a few years ago that my dad writes better than he talks.

"No, I'm okay," I assure him. "Just girl stuff, you know." I put my hand on my stomach to make it look like I have cramps. This shuts him up instantly; he nods quickly and begins hunting for unpopped kernels inside the bowl.

I put him out of his misery by asking him about the book he's currently working on: a story about a man who walks the historic Camino de Santiago trail in Spain with a three-legged dog and a burned-out Norwegian heavy metal musician named Lars. Dad reaches for the black binder on the table beside him and reads me a few passages. I love it when he reads his work to me. He gets all animated and does an amazing job of using different voices for his characters. I always end up laughing, and tonight I could do with some laughing.

While he reads me the chapter where Michael, the protagonist, gets sick from drinking too much cheap sherry, there is suddenly a loud "boom," and the radio inside in the kitchen goes silent. The fire alarm beeps twice from its home on the living room ceiling: a sure sign the power has gone out.

"That's strange," Dad says, shuffling the papers on his lap. "There's not a puff of wind out there tonight. Wonder what happened?"

"An accident, maybe?" We both sit on the deck, finishing the last of the popcorn, and listen for a siren that doesn't come.

I turn around and check the neighbouring docks. It doesn't look like anyone has power, although a couple of boats can be heard firing up noisy generators.

"Well," Dad says, "on that note, I guess we call it a night." He gets up and stubs his toe on the leg of his chair on his way to the door. "Aggghh . . . ffffffish-hooks-it! I hate doing that!"

I would have thought he'd be used to it by now, seeing as he does it on a regular basis, usually with more colourful language, and much hopping around. Dad can be quite dramatic.

An hour later, it's dark, and my already scratchy eyes feel even worse from straining to see the entries in my diary. I'm just about to blow out the candle when my cell phone pings. No one has texted me for a million years, and by no one, of course, I mean Max. I reach inside, slide it open, and wait while the screen lights up. Yep. It's him.

Hey Anderson. Your power out, 2?

I force myself to wait a whole minute before I text him back: Yup. Whole marina is out.

Two seconds later he answers. Max has great keyboarding skills. X-box.

Hey, can U meet me right now?

I hesitate. Now? Who does he think he is?

Why?

Will tell U when I see U. But it's important.

Nah. 2 L8.

Don't B weird, Han. Just meet me in 10, ok? Bring your bike.

This makes me furious. Does he think I'm going to drop

everything for him? I'm just supposed to forget everything he said to me and follow his orders? What a control freak!

Well?

Am 2 tired.

I know my response is what Aunt Maddie would refer to as "passive-aggressive," but whatever.

Fine. Will have 2 deal w/ eagle by myself. TTYL.

What???

A bald eagle was killed right near my place.

That's all it takes for me to forget that I'm mad at Max. Animals in trouble.

What do U mean? What happened?

Can't talk now. Meet in 10, OK? U R the only 1 who gets it, Y know?

(*I know.*)

Where shud we meet?

Blue Moon Kayaks?

Ok. OMW.

Cool. U rock.

I rock. Either that, or I'm a complete sucker for punishment.

Dad is the best. When I ask him if I can run out at ten o'clock on a Tuesday night in the midst of a power outage because of an animal in distress, he simply hands me a flashlight, gives me a hug, and tells me to be back ASAP. A lot of parents would tell their fourteen-year-old daughter to forget it, but my dad is all about taking action.

Blue Moon Kayak Rentals sits at the end of the village, just a few minutes past the row of stores that run along the shoreline. When I ride past the pottery studio, I see Max up ahead, leaning against the stack of rental boats just outside the building's main door. I know it's him because of his signature slouch. Ever since he grew to be 5' 10" he's developed one. Probably from constantly bumping into things he isn't used to bumping into.

He straightens a little when he sees me, and I shut off the flashlight. I can't believe I feel this awkward standing in front of my best friend.

"Hey," he says.

"Hey," I say back.

"Thanks for coming."

"Sure."

And then we both say "Um" at the same time.

"Oh," I say, "you first."

"Well," he twists the ball cap, the one he seems to wear all the time now, farther down on his head. "I've been thinking a lot lately, and I just need to tell you that you were wrong, Hannah."

"What do you mean?" My face starts to burn.

"About Sabrina. You were wrong about Sabrina. I didn't tell her about what you did two summers ago."

I don't say anything.

"So, that's all I have to say. Either you believe me, or you don't. Actually, I'm kind of pissed off that you'd think I'd lie to you. That's not what a real friend would do."

I think about what he says. "Okay, but I guess it works both ways. I could say exactly the same thing to you. Either you believe me about what happened then, or you don't."

He looks thoughtful. "Fair enough. You're right. I'm sorry."

"So you believe me?" I have to know. I have to know if Max thinks I'm crazy. But he doesn't say yes or no. Instead he reaches for my hand and squeezes it.

"I hate fighting with you. I'm really sorry."

"I'm sorry, too. It's just—"

"It's okay," he interrupts. "I can understand why you would think I told her. But I have no idea how she found out about all that stuff. Really. Can we just drop it now? Can we just be normal again? And can I tell you about the eagle now?"

He's right. We need to drop it. It doesn't matter. I know what's real, and that's what counts.

"It took the power out," he says, standing up straight. His head almost touches the bow of a bright green kayak poking out from the rack.

"What? The eagle?" How does a bird knock out power?

"I saw it happen. I was taking Tucker out for a pee and I saw this massive bald eagle swoop down and pick up a rabbit," he says, talking faster and faster. "He just snapped it off the ground and then tried to fly over the road, and then bam! Straight into the hydro line!"

I remember the loud boom that Dad and I heard earlier on the deck.

"Is it okay?"

"No," Max says solemnly. "It died. Electrocuted. Dropped out of the sky and hit the ground hard. I went over and shone my Maglite on it. It's weird because it only has a small burn mark on its leg. The rabbit got completely frazzled, though."

"What do we do? Where is it?"

"It's just up there." Max points. "On the side of the road. We have to move it before something happens to it. Mom said you have to notify the conservation officer about eagle carcasses, because they're protected. The Bald and Golden Eagle Protection Act or, something. I can't remember exactly. Anyway, we have to move it."

"Okay, let's go."

While we walk up the hill, Max tells me the story all over again. I am reminded of the first time I met him, two years ago in grade six when he was a new kid just arrived from Williams Lake. The first conversation we ever had was about animals. He had been drawing a fish and a hummingbird on the front of his duo-tang. He was, and still is, an amazing artist.

"There," he says, pointing to a spot on the side of the road. "See?"

I follow his finger with my flashlight and see the smooth white head of the eagle lying motionless on the pavement. My heart jumps in my chest. Now that I'm here I'm not sure I want to see this.

He steps away from the bird and I get a better look. I've never seen an eagle up close before, and it's massive. One of its wings is folded close to its body and the other bent at an awkward angle. I squat down closer, and then take a step away when I see the charred remains of the cottontail rabbit, a pretty common sight around this part of the island, still locked in one of the eagle's talons. It's a gruesome sight, but I feel sadder for the eagle than I do for the rabbit, especially when Max tells me that it was probably bringing dinner to a nearby nest.

"One of my mom's birdy friends told me that eagles don't carry heavy prey around unless there's a nest close by. It's too much work. I guess this one couldn't clear the line in time. You wouldn't know it from what's left of it, but that rabbit was actually a pretty decent size. So there's probably a nest around here."

"Where *is* your mom?" I ask. It's a good question. Max's mom is a serious bird freak. The Millers' house is filled with coffee-table bird books and field guides. She even has a fancy birdcall app on her iPhone. She'd be all over this.

"She's out at the cabin till late tonight. I tried calling her but cell service is so sketchy in Sahtlam. Dad's in Victoria, but he doesn't know a bird's arse from its face, anyway. Come on, we have to get this eagle off the road now."

But just when we're about to pick up the lifeless bird, someone screams from the bottom of the hill. We jump to our feet.

"What was that?" I say, my heart thumping like a jackhammer in my chest. There's another scream, followed by a shrill, *"Please! Help!"*

We don't hesitate. We both jump on Mathilda, doubling down the hill old-school-style, way faster than we should. I squeeze my eyes shut and hope that we don't hit any potholes or wayward cats or startled deer, and cling to Max's sides in a death grip until we pass by the front windows of Blue Moon Kayaks again.

The scream, we discover, is coming from Sabrina Webber. She is standing in the middle of the parking lot, clutching her hands to her heart, while a few flashlight-wielding night staff from the Gangplank Pub surround her.

"Sabrina?" Max says, surprised. He brakes so hard that I smack full on into the back of him and knock him off balance.

"Ouch!" he says, steadying himself while switching on his flashlight.

"Sorry," I say, even though it was his fault.

"Are you okay?" A guy in a pair of black pants and a white shirt steps forward toward Sabrina, looking concerned. He's wearing a name badge on his shirt that says "Russ." Behind him are two waitresses but I can't read their nametags. It's too dark.

"Oh my God! It was totally a cougar!" Sabrina squeaks breathlessly, fanning a hand in front of her face. "Right over there!" She points across the road toward a thicket of alder trees.

"He came out behind that car and looked right at me!" Sabrina makes a grab for Max's arm as though she might faint and fall over. "I'm sure it was going to attack me!"

"You're sure?" Russ asks, looking dubious. "You're sure it was a cougar?"

Sabrina lets go of Max's arm and hooks both thumbs on the jeweled belt slung low on her hips. "Well, duh!" she says. "Hello? I'm not an idiot. I think I know what a cougar looks like!"

Russ doesn't say anything, but he doesn't look convinced either.

"What are you doing out here anyway?" Max asks. The same thing had occurred to me, but the less conversation I have with Sabrina Webber, the better.

"My mom and my uncle and I were having dinner in there, but then the power went out," she explains. "I wanted to leave, but my uncle had to go off to do some stupid business thing, and now my mom doesn't want to go." Sabrina turns her head and scowls at the oversized porthole windows of the Gangplank, then looks back to Max. "She's totally flirting with the waiters and stuff. It's *so* embarrassing, you know? She's like, forty. No. Wait. She's actually forty-one. I don't even want to think about it. So anyway, I said I was going to go wait in the car, but then I saw it! Oh my God! It was massive! I totally could have died!"

"Doubtful," I can't resist saying. "Cougar attacks are pretty rare."

She suddenly notices me on the back of the bike and her eyes go all slitty. "*Awww* . . . you guys made up. How cute."

Just then, there is a noise from across the road. One of the waitresses shines her flashlight at some tawny fur that appears between two of the parked cars.

Sabrina lets loose with a scream that could wake the dead, and I cover my ears even though I'm still wearing my helmet.

"IT'S GOING TO KILL US!" she screeches.

There is more movement, and then the beast shows itself, walking out between the cars to stand in the middle of the road. I can't help it. I start laughing. A lot. Because it's no cougar, it's not even close. It's Quincy. He wags his back end as he trots over, and then he pushes his nose against the back pocket of my jeans, looking for the milk bone dog biscuits he usually finds there.

"Well, I guess he's sort of the same colour as a cougar," Max says, trying hard not to laugh. Russ and the two waitresses just shake their heads and go back into the restaurant, clearly annoyed.

"And you can tell my mom that it's just awesome that she cares so much about her daughter's welfare!" Sabrina yells after them. She turns back to us and sneers at Quincy who has given up on my pockets and is now sniffing Max's shoes. "So what? Anyone could have made the same mistake."

"Oh, absolutely," I say earnestly, adding, "especially the tail part. Cougars have such long, distinctive ones." This is not a very sympathetic thing to say, because Quincy's tail is just a small, hairy stump that vibrates 24/7.

"Shut up, Hannah," Sabrina says sullenly.

Thankfully, Max's dopey grin disappears when he looks up the hill and remembers the eagle. "Well, glad you're okay," he tells Sabrina, "but we kind of have to go. I guess we'll see you tomorrow. Last day of school!"

Control your enthusiasm, Miller.

"Yeah," I say, "and I wouldn't advise going out in the woods carrying kitty treats or anything."

Sabrina doesn't bother to say anything. Instead, she turns angrily and flounces back toward the Gangplank, her high-heeled sandals clacking on the pavement as she goes.

"Be nice, Hannah," Max says under his breath. I notice that he's still watching Sabrina walk away.

"Why?" I believe it to be a fair question.

Before he can answer, a black Hummer pulls up in front of the Gangplank's door. The headlights beam across the entire parking lot.

"Go get your mom, Sabrina! I have stuff to do," says the man behind the wheel. He has movie star hair and must be wearing a lot of cologne because I can smell it from ten feet away.

"Finally!" Sabrina scowls. "What took you so long? Way to ditch us, Uncle Ray!"

Ray? Why does that name sound familiar?

Sabrina turns and goes into the Gangplank, slamming the pub's door behind her.

Sabrina's uncle smiles a toothy grin directly at Max. "Women!" he says, shaking his head.

"Come on," Max says, looking at me through the glare of

the Hummer's high beams. "Let's go."

When we get to the side of the road and Max offers to push Mathilda up the hill, I don't argue. I can't remember ever feeling this tired.

We're halfway up when headlights appear at the crest of the hill. A truck flies by, heading for the village, spraying loose gravel as it passes. I recognize the white canopy and fog lights. It's that red 4x4 again—the one that almost backed into me by the hardware store.

When we reach the spot on the side of the road, I just stand there and blink stupidly at the bare ground. It takes a few seconds for my head to clear, and when it does I can't believe what I'm *not* seeing.

Max and I stare at each other in the dark, and then scan the ground in every direction. But all we see is a tire track in the gravel, and a few random feathers. The eagle is gone.

"Wait," Max whispers, grabbing my arm. "Do you smell that?"

I sniff the air and there is a faint, sweet smell that I recognize right away. Everyone knows what pot smells like, and even thought it's dark I swear I can see smoke hanging in the air around us.

A chill runs through me and I shiver. Something is going on in Cowichan Bay, and my gut tells me it isn't good.

Chapter Ten

❧

IZZY

I SIT ON THE CORNER of the bed in the cabin that Ramona has prepared for my stay here. It's not really a cabin. It's more of a glorified garden shed. A kind of ramshackle outbuilding that sits near a slightly larger one she uses for her studio. Mine sits at the bottom of the sloping lawn, alongside a rickety dock leading out to a spit of sand at the shoreline. There are three paned windows running up beside a white painted door with another paned window at the top. A braided rug sits on the wooden plank floor in front of my bed, and on top of the drop-leaf table against the wall is a vase of flowers—tiny yellow ones I don't recognize, which isn't surprising. I'm not really the flower type.

"It's not much," Ramona had said when Mom and I arrived and I'd heaved my duffle bag up on the bed, "but you'll have a bit of privacy in the evenings, and in the daytime . . . well, you'll mostly be with me in the studio just up the path."

It had been a long day, made even longer after Mom decided to hang around so she and Ramona could "catch up."

I spent most of the morning with my shadow—literally—and reading down on the dock, not that I retained any of the words on the page.

When I got sick of my book, I wandered back up to the deck by the cabin. We'd seen kayaks sitting on the grass next to the dock, and I wanted to check them out. Mom had gone gaga when she'd spotted them. "Oh look, Iz! Kayaks! You'll be able to explore the estuary! Isn't that great? You like birds!"

Thanks for reminding me, Mom. I might have forgotten.

"You'll find extra blankets in the box under your bed," Ramona had said, trying to break the tension. "There's often a bit of a breeze off the water, so sometimes it gets a little chilly at night."

Not surprising when you have to sleep in a drafty garden shed!

The only not-so-crappy thing about having to spend the summer at Salish Sea Studio turns out to be Paco and Luna, the resident alpacas that Ramona keeps in the field at the side of her house. I notice their shelter is much bigger than mine. But they really are cool-looking animals, and Luna's pure white fleece is soft and bright against Paco's chocolate brown coat.

It isn't long before Mom and Ramona appear and lean

against the fence on either side of me—they've been joined at the hip since we got here. "Luna was shorn a couple of months ago," Ramona explains as I stroke the soft, long neck. "It was her first time, and, oh, you should have seen it! Such a beautiful white cria fleece. Everybody wanted to buy it."

"Cria fleece?" I say, despite my resolve to stay silent.

"Baby alpaca fleece. The first shearing is always the most sought-after because it's so beautiful and soft. And Luna's was *so* white. Gorgeous! I should have saved some for you, Louise," Ramona says to my mom.

Paco, who turns up his lip to display a row of long and yellow teeth, pushes Luna out of the way and comes in for a scratch.

"Paco's needy," Ramona laughs. "He likes to be the centre of attention."

I bury my fingertips in the soft, thick fleece and he curls up the corner of his lip.

"Listen. I'm going to go and have a bite to eat with your mom before she goes," Ramona says, flipping her long braid over her shoulder. It's mostly black, but with more silver running through it than I remember. "Come join us? We have yogurt pie."

I shrug. "No thanks."

"Suit yourself." They walk back up the hill toward the cottage, their arms linked together as they chatter away about the medicinal properties of cottonwood buds. Small things amuse small minds, I guess.

"Some happy hour," I mutter to the alpacas after they've gone. "Rosehip tea and fake cheesecake with Ramona and Mom. I'll pass." But after spending twenty minutes engaged in a one-sided conversation with my new hairy companions, my stomach betrays me and begins to growl. I remember that all I've eaten today is a cookie.

I tiptoe in through the back door to Ramona's kitchen, and see Mom sitting in a wicker chair on the porch at the front of the house. She's holding a red coffee mug in her hands, and a piece of the pie sits on a plate in her lap.

Well, maybe just a slice, I decide. Then I'll return to my garden shed to stare at the cobwebs in the corners until it gets dark.

"I'm so grateful for this, Ramona," Mom says. "I just don't know what to do with her anymore."

I stop in my tracks and duck in behind the oak wardrobe in the narrow hallway.

"She's welcome to stay here as long as she likes, Lou. And if she takes to working at the studio, well, it's a win-win, right? Besides, I'm happy for selfish reasons, too. I could sure use the help."

"Lots of orders?" Mom asks.

"Sweaters, mostly," Ramona says, "and some slippers, too."

Ah yes, the famous Cowichan sweater. Our claim to fame.

"Well that's great!"

Within minutes their conversation turns to—big surprise —wool and a recipe for some kind of natural red dye, and then the best way to steam stinging nettles in the spring for some kind of foul-smelling hair rinse.

I've heard these kinds of conversations a million times before, and know that it's only a matter of time before they start talking about the old ways: eating bark and berries, and tracking animals—all that "one-with-the-earth" stuff. But the worst part is when Mom gets all stoked about the legends: those embarrassing stories about shape-shifting and talking bears and people falling out of the sky. How anyone could believe in all that crap is a mystery to me. Mom takes the cake, though. She likes to trot those tales out at the most inappropriate times. Parent-teacher interviews, the dentist's office, and especially when my friends are over. Dylan and Jess usually act like they're interested—sometimes they even ask questions—but I'm pretty sure they're just being polite. Get this: Mom has even enlightened strangers in the lineup at the grocery store! Doesn't she know how foolish she sounds?

I creep back out through the kitchen and into the back yard, snatching a piece of the yogurt pie out of the plate on the counter as I go. The afternoon sun sparkles on the water and, when I reach the dock, a kingfisher dive-bombs the surface a little farther down in the estuary. This feels better than being stuck in the cottage, listening to that non-stop chatter. Quiet is good.

Mom talked the entire way over from Salt Spring, and when she'd seen a big raven circling above the ferry deck as we docked, she took it upon herself to trot out her family's famous "magic bird" story . . . *again*! It's her favourite: about a white girl with flaming red hair who supposedly time-travelled from the future, together with her magic raven, back to the 1860s, right in Cowichan Bay.

I must have heard it a million times, especially the part about how Mom's great-granny-times-six and the white girl ran away from Sasquatches and sailors, all because of some stupid spindle whorl or something. I think maybe my grandma accidentally dropped my mom on her head when she was a baby. I mean, *come on*!

My thoughts are interrupted by a loud screech coming from somewhere high up in the trees. I look above me and see an eagle perched way up on a branch, its white head a beacon in the afternoon sun. It looks down at me and makes clipped little "screes" and then hops into a more dense area of fir trees where it disappears altogether.

I walk back up the dock and stop in the shadow of a big stand of firs. The eagle stops calling just long enough for me to hear another noise—this one fainter and more frantic. I've heard these sounds before. Eaglets. I know this because of my cousin Victor, who is an eagle fanatic. He carves them. Photographs them. Watches them, and his house in Port Renfrew is full of all things "eagle." It's kind of an obsession, I guess. I spent a whole summer up there a few years ago. I've had worse times than I had that summer at Port Renfrew, I guess.

The mature bird suddenly hurtles from the treetops and soars out over the ocean. It circles a few times, big wide arcs over the water, before returning to the tangle of fir boughs where it makes the same piercing, staccato "screes" again.

And like it or not, I know that those cries are the cries of a worried parent.

I return to the end of the dock, scanning the sky and the beach for the eagle's mate, but all I see are a bunch of pigeons and a scruffy looking seagull. I head back to the trees.

"Izzy?" It's Ramona, at the kitchen door.

"Yeah?"

"Your mom is leaving! Come say bye!"

I sigh. Time for the "emotional goodbye." I trudge back up the boardwalk toward the cottage.

"Lemme see that beautiful smile, Isabelle," Mom says as she settles herself in our van.

I give her a giant, toothy grimace. I can't help it. Does she have to be so damn positive all the time?

"Hope you know what you're in for," Mom says through clenched teeth to Ramona, who has draped her arm around my shoulder as though we're suddenly BFFs. I want to shrug it off, but force myself to stay still. Making a little scene could delay Mom's departure, and she and her ever-cheery smile need to hit the road sooner rather than later, thank you very much.

"Oh, I think I can handle a teenager who thinks she's got all the answers," Ramona chuckles. "I remember being fifteen." She winks at me as if we're both hardcore rebels. I want to scream.

"Now you call me anytime, sweetie," Mom says while she adjusts the rearview mirror. "Amelia and I are sure going to miss you."

Then why send me here?

Ramona and I stand at the side of the road and watch the van pull away. Mom honks the horn twice and then vanishes around the bend.

My "vacation" has officially begun.

Chapter Eleven

TODAY IS THE FINAL day of school but we have to spend it doing things like returning textbooks, getting our report cards, buying our yearbooks and tying up "loose ends," whatever that means. The teachers are burned out but I guess by law they have to hold us captive until two o'clock. I'm pretty sure that's why we end up watching movies all morning.

I'm grateful to sit in front of a big TV screen and not think about things that will make my head hurt. I'm still rattled from the whole "disappearing eagle" thing, but Max made me promise not to say anything to anyone about it. Not yet, anyway. "There's no sense stirring the pot until you have all the ingredients," he said, another one of his old-man expressions.

But the fact is, there's probably a nest of starving eaglets nearby with only one parent around to keep them fed. Eagle chicks have to eat a lot, and often, and that is a huge job for a single parent. Max and I need to get this last day of school over with!

In math class, Mrs. Rickman appears to have forgotten that we are all teenagers, and sticks us in front of Walt Disney's animated classic, *Cinderella*. Of course, no one complains, because doing so would have us cleaning counters and washing all the geometry sets with rags and a bucket of Lysol. Mrs. Rickman is a total germaphobe. I've never seen so many bottles of hand sanitizer in a classroom before. So yeah, I'm quite happy to watch Cinderella do the cleaning and sweeping, while I try not to stress about baby eagles, lunatics in the woods, and, to a slightly lesser degree, the fact that I've caught Max looking at Sabrina twice this morning.

When we get to the part where Cinderella is being decorated like a Christmas tree by those squeaky, stickpin-wielding mice, there's a noise at the window. I jump, and turn to see Jack rapping madly on the glass with his beak.

"Oh!" Mrs. Rickman says.

There is something sticking out of the side of Jack's beak. Oh please! Not another lame gift. I sink lower in my chair in an attempt to disappear.

"Hey!" someone from the front of the room says. That someone has a high-pitched, irritating voice and giggles more often than is necessary. That someone is, of course, Sabrina. "Isn't that Hannah Anderson's little bird friend?"

I glare at her, and pray that the Patron Saint of Just Desserts will intervene and make her perfect trendy up-do come undone, tangle in her chair, and have to be hacked off with scissors, but no such luck. Instead, a breeze blows through the partially open window and rearranges her wavy blonde tendrils artfully around her face. I swear any moment the violin and harp music will start up.

"Look!" she continues, pointing. "He's totally trying to come in the window!"

Oh, *pleeease*! This can't be true. I will Jack to take off and go squawk his little heart out in some far-away tree like a regular raven, but he seems very intent—almost frantic—about getting my attention. When he hunkers down like a demented, feathery limbo dancer and hops right on in under the window sash, I know he means business.

"Jack! Go away!" I yell. My cheeks grow hot and I close my eyes. Rats. Busted.

"Seriously? You *named* him?" Sabrina giggles. "Did you guys hear that? She named him! His name is Jack!"

Mrs. Rickman is over to the window like a shot, swatting at Jack with a rolled up Scholastic book order flyer. "Go!" she flaps nervously. "Go on! Shoo, you filthy bird!" But Jack hops from a stack of textbooks to a ceramic pot full of African violets, to Megan Corrie's desk. Megan leaps into the air as though a giant cockroach has just attacked her. Mrs. Rickman looks close to passing out.

Jack travels from desk to desk, and the other kids spring from their seats to jump around after him like a pack of wild, sugar-high pre-schoolers. It's horrible, like a scene out of *Lord of the Flies*. Most of the class thinks this is the funniest thing in the world, and I realize that Jack has gone from excited to petrified in a matter of seconds. He is soon cornered next to the fish tanks, his eyes wild and staring. In the two years I've known him, I've never seen him look like this. Not even that first summer when the Thumquas chased us!

Brady Hart and Mark Lukovich creep closer, wildly flapping their arms in a crappy imitation of flight. Jack is beside himself. He loses his footing near the fish tanks and pitches to the polished floor, letting out a pathetic caw.

"STOP IT!" I yell, pushing past Brady and Mark. I face them, standing in front of Jack with my arms spread out protectively on either side. "Get away from him! You're scaring him!" I'm not one for making scenes, but seeing Jack this frightened makes me crazy.

"Hannah," Mrs. Rickman says, trying to sound in control, "you need to calm down. I'm going to call Mr. Talbot. He'll know how to get rid of—"

"NO!" I yell, and the room grows silent. Not Mr. Talbot! He may be a good janitor but he hates animals. He brags about using his pellet gun on the stellar jays, plus I've seen him hose stray dogs that cross through the soccer field. "Don't get Mr. Talbot! I'll deal with it!"

"Hannah! That bird is clearly distressed, and probably disease-ridden! I'm not going—"

"Mrs. Rickman," I plead, taking a deep breath. "Sabrina is right. I do sort of know this bird. I can take him back outside. Please. If everyone could just stay still, I can get him out of here."

And then Max does a great thing. He gets up on a table and puts a hand out in the air in front of him. "Okay listen!" he says to the rest of the class like he's totally in control, even though I know he's nervous because his ears are red. "Hannah knows what she's doing here so everyone just quit freaking the bird out! Please just sit down and Hannah will take him outside."

And just like that, everyone does.

I smile gratefully at Max, and turn to face Jack. He's on the ground near the old *Encyclopedia Britannica* volumes, and I move slowly toward him, keeping my voice to a whisper.

"It's okay, Jack. I'm here. Come on, buddy. Hop on." I crouch down, holding my arm out straight in front of me, and he looks at it and then past my shoulders to everyone now sitting at their desks. Even Mrs. Rickman stands totally still in a corner of the room, leaning against the life-sized plastic human skeleton we all call Mr. Bones.

"Come on," I urge softly. "You can trust me. You know you can." I am calm, and I realize that I don't care anymore who hears me. I just want to help Jack. His feathers are all ruffled up and his beak is open. He takes a hesitant step forward, and then two more and then he's up on my forearm. I hardly feel the weight of him as I stand. Despite appearances, he is only about two pounds.

"That's it, buddy," I tell him, walking slowly toward the door at the back of the classroom. "It's okay, don't be scared." Jack's feet grip my arm so tightly that one of his talons pokes a hole through my sleeve.

As soon as we reach the door, he takes off back to the open window, picks something up in his beak, and then returns to my outstretched arm. I tiptoe outside, away from the chaos, my heart beating triple time. Now I see what Jack is holding in his beak, what he *had* to retrieve from the window ledge. I hold out my other hand and he carefully places the object in my open palm.

It's a feather.

An eagle feather.

❧

"Something's going on in the Bay and I think it involves the *Orca I*," I tell Max at lunch hour. We're eating on the bleachers by the track, watching Kyle Graham, the fastest kid in the school, run laps, even though our track meet was last week and P.E. is a pretty much over for the year.

"Do you suppose he's always been that fast?" Max asks, his eyes fixated on Kyle.

"Huh?"

"Kyle. Do you think he ran fast like that when he was a little kid?"

"Sure. Maybe. I don't know. Anyway." I pull out my apple. "The *Orca I*. Jack goes out there all the time, and when the power went out, I swear I saw a light in one of the lower windows." I take a bite of the apple and make a face. It's the kind that you think will be delicious because it's hard and crunchy, but turns out to be all woody and gross when you bite into it.

"I heard Sabrina's uncle may have got the salvage rights," Max offers.

"Really? It's been floating out there for over three years."

"I guess."

"Also, I . . . don't laugh, okay?" I say.

"I won't laugh."

"Well, I think I saw two people in a boat beside it. At like 4:30 in the morning! It was foggy, but I think—" I stop. I sound crazy, even to myself.

"I'm listening. What else?" Max says, still watching Kyle.

"Well, I keep thinking about the weird stuff that Jack keeps bringing me." I look for a raven in the trees at the far end of the track, but there's no sign of Jack. "I mean, was the feather he gave me a feather from *our* eagle? Does it have something to do with the beer cap and the bear claw?"

I can't tell if Max is listening.

"And," I say, "why is he so frenzied these days? Can ravens have Type A personalities? Because if they can, Jack is quickly becoming the poster bird."

"Yeah," Max agrees, "I guess."

"Anyway," I continue, "I think it's all related somehow. I think he's trying to tell me something."

"Hmmmm," Max mumbles. "Maybe. You figure he has to follow a special diet or anything?"

"Who? Jack?"

"No. Kyle."

"MAX!"

"What?" He looks at me as though I'm the one who's act-ing strange.

"You're not helping," I tell him.

"Not helping with what?"

"Are you even listening to me?" I pitch my woody apple far across the field, where it lands by the bike racks. Some rac-coon will have a midnight dessert tonight.

"Nice toss, Han," Max says, clearly impressed.

"Listen! I'm talking about the *Orca I*," I say. "I think we should go and investigate. Check it out from the water. We can paddle out in the kayaks."

"Forget it, Anderson. We have a nest to find before we check out any derelict boats," Max says. "You gotta focus, girl! Think stuff through." He pulls out a bag of dried apricots and offers me some. "Besides, that boat is a heap. It's not safe. And we'd be trespassing."

"We were snooping around that property by Whitetail Farm," I remind him. "And what about that weird garbage we found there. Don't you think that's suspicious?" I reach into the bag and help myself to a few of the apricots. I hate it when Max thinks he can start calling all the shots. He never used to be like this, only since he got so tall and buff. Does he think I'm stupid or something? "Never mind," I say curtly, "I'll just go by myself."

Max rolls his eyes. "Hannah, that old tub is so locked up.

Besides, I hear it's pretty gross out there. Riley and Ben say there are a million pigeons roosting on it, and it's covered in bird crap and barnacles."

"So you're wussing out on me? When did you become such a giant chicken?"

"What? No! It's not that. I'm just trying to protect you from—"

"I don't need you to protect me," I say, sitting up straighter. "I just need you to help me. But if you're too chicken I'll just—"

"Okay! Okay! I'll go with you in a few days, okay?"

"You will? Really?" I smile. *Score.*

"I just said I would," he says impatiently, "but eagles first, okay?"

"Yes! Of course. I want to find them, too. I just have a bad feeling about that boat, that's all." I crinkle up the saran wrap from my sandwich and stuff it into the bottom of my pack.

Max picks up the eagle feather from where it sits between us and studies it carefully. "Man, we weren't even gone ten minutes. Someone had to have been watching us the whole time. Someone who wanted that bird."

"I know, and that truck. The red 4x4."

"Yeah, I know."

"Pretty sure it's the same one that was at the hardware store," I say, thinking about the guys loading the bags of potting soil.

"Maybe," Max says, and then he grins. "Hey. Sabrina sure was freaked out."

"I know," I say. "Not the sharpest tool in the shed, I guess."

"Oh, go easy on her, Han. She doesn't know any better. She's not exactly a nature-lover, you know?"

And then, as if on cue, Sabrina appears on the stairs between the bleachers, in a different outfit from the one she had on this morning. This time she's wearing short shorts, a two-sizes too small white, cropped t-shirt, and wedge sandals. She does what I'm sure she thinks is a "model walk" out onto the field and then begins to demonstrate her impressive flexibility by doing a series of complex yoga stretches. Kyle Graham's running slows to a conservative jog.

"What a ditz," I say, feeling mean.

When Max doesn't answer, I look over and see him staring at her, a dried apricot halfway to his face in his frozen hand.

I hate Sabrina Webber.

❦

Eventually the bell rings and we're officially free. Most kids hang around waiting to get their yearbooks signed, but Max and I are at the school bus before anyone else, anxious to get dropped off just past the village and start our nest-hunting quest.

By the time bus driver appears, there is a long line of kids waiting to board the bus, but even after everyone is on, it takes him forever to start the engine. First he shuffles papers around on his dashboard, then he rearranges his lumbar support cushion, and then he fiddles with the lid on his travel mug for what seems like an eternity. I can't help fidgeting in my seat. Why is it that when you're in a hurry, the entire world conspires to slow you down?

To make matters worse, when we reach Cowichan Bay Road, we get stuck behind an elderly lady in a brown station wagon, doing 25k an hour. Then when Michael Park makes the driver stop the bus because he says he's going to puke, I start chewing my fingernails. We wait for five minutes while he stands just outside the bus door looking green and clutching his stomach, but he never throws up. I think about that probable nest of starving eaglets getting hungrier and hungrier by the minute.

When we finally arrive at our stop, we walk over and lean against the old split-rail fence bordering Maple Grove Park by the estuary, carefully avoiding the tangle of clematis blooms that cover most of the wood.

"So," I say, "where do we go first?" It's hard to know how or where to start.

"I think we just listen, and watch for the other parent eagle." Max says this matter-of-factly. "Maybe we should walk out to the look-out." He points to the raised wooden viewing platform near the ocean. It's across what the locals call Trumpeter's Field, because of the swans that migrate there every year, but it's an awesome walk out there. The pathway runs alongside the briny water where the sea meets up with the mouth of the Cowichan and the Koksilah Rivers. Max's mom says the estuary is home to two hundred species of birds.

Ten minutes later we've climbed the stairs to the platform, and are looking back to the shoreline, across the finger of water that cuts through the wetland. The hum of traffic on Cowichan Bay Road isn't too bad, so it's easy to listen for any telltale bird sounds. There are lots. A red-winged blackbird calls from a clump of cattails at the edge of the field, and the high-pitched titter of a kingfisher sounds from the other side of the dyke.

We don't speak, turning in all directions, listening, and watching for anything that might sound a little out of the ordinary.

Chapter Twelve

❦

IZZY

"NOW YOU JUST MAKE yourself at home, Isabelle," Ramona says after Mom leaves. "I have to run out for a bit but I won't be long."

"Sure thing." Being alone will be the best thing that's happened to me since I got here.

"Just a couple of stops. Some bread and maybe some of Nell's granola cookies? You'll love them! Everyone does. Unless of course they're all snapped up by the time I get there. They're usually gone by lunch, but I guess I could always pick up some banana bread. I mean, who doesn't like banana bread, right?"

I look at her and nod, but really, I'm not thinking about banana bread. I'm thinking how strange it is that Ramona doesn't regularly pass out from forgetting to breathe when she talks. Between her and my mother . . .

"So," she goes on, buckling the straps of her Birkenstock sandals, "who knows what I'll come home with, but I also need to stop by the bookstore and pick up some good reads they put aside for me. One of them is sure to interest you, Izzy. It's all about Coast Salish art, and knitting and what not. You'll be completely mesmerized with it. I know I was, especially the part about the history of the Cowichan sweater! Did you know our people used to keep little poodle-type dogs in their camps and spin wool from their coats? Can you imagine such a thing?" Ramona takes a deep breath and places her hands on her ample hips.

"*Our people*?" I say flatly. "I take it you aren't referring to your Scottish roots?"

"Well," Ramona says hesitantly, "no, I wasn't. Although the Scottish *are* known for their Shetland ponies, aren't they, but I don't suppose anyone ever tried knitting a sweater out of horsehair. Now *that* would be itchy! But come to think of it, they did invent the Fair Isle sweater. Very intricate knitting. I made one once. Almost went mad! It took me an entire winter. All those colour changes and such a detailed yoke."

"Ramona? I'm kind of tired," I tell her, changing the subject. It isn't a lie. I feel like I could sleep for twenty-four hours straight. "I think I'll go and lie down for a while."

"Oh!" Ramona says. She takes a cloth shopping bag from a hook beside the door and folds it into the pocket of her long skirt. "That's a very good idea. Everyone just loves that little hut, what with a nice ocean breeze and everything. I won't wake you when I get back. Promise. You just relax, and like I said, make yourself at home. I'll be quiet as a mouse."

After Ramona goes, I lie on my back on the thick foam mattress in my cabin, while the breeze coming off the sea blows through the open door. I can smell salt and sun, and it's not an altogether bad smell. Different somehow from Salt Spring sea air, even though it's just a hop across the Sansum Narrows.

I sneak a cigarette, shoving the pack in behind two books on the shelf near the bed, and when I finish I snuff out the butt in the hardened dirt of an old flowerpot on the windowsill.

A few minutes later, I have trouble keeping my eyes open, and it isn't long before I let my neck relax and sink back heavily into the soft feather pillow behind my head. I wonder what my friends are doing? I bet they've gone into Ganges or something to celebrate. I force the image out of my head.

When I wake up, I'm disoriented. I've been dreaming but I can't remember what the dream was about. The forest. And animal sounds. Birds, I think.

I sit up. How long have I been sleeping? Minutes or hours? I blink several times and shake my head. I couldn't have been out for long, even though it seems like it.

Waves are lapping at the shoreline, and the door hangs ajar just as it was earlier. Last month's *Cowichan Bay Herald* lies on the table next to the bed, and I pick it up, looking at the article that takes up half of the front page.

HIKERS MAKE GRISLY DISCOVERY NEAR YOUBOU
Slaughtered Roosevelt Elk Evidence of Poaching

A large photograph shows six slain elk, all bulls, with their antlers gone. I scan the article, reading something about the black market and how elk antler velvet is so valuable. It makes me want to hurl. People do such horrible things for money. It makes me especially angry when animals are involved, I guess maybe because they are such innocent victims. Sometimes I wonder how we got to be at the top of the food chain.

I push the paper away, and at the same time I hear a high-pitched sound overhead, the same noise I heard earlier.

I swing my legs over the side of the bed, cross the weathered planks to the entranceway, and step out onto the bleached boards of the deck. The noise stops, and I stand with my head tipped back to the sky, watching for movement. It isn't long before the tree branches shake, and the eagle I saw earlier appears again in a flurry of motion, its white head brilliant against the cloudless blue backdrop of sky. It circles the tree for several moments, banks left, and is out of sight almost immediately. Where did it go? Now there is a softer sound: short, staccato cries that reinforce what I suspected earlier. There *are* chicks. Hungry ones!

I walk across the dock and stop under the stand of firs on the grass. I can't see anything, but then again, I don't expect to. The nest would be well hidden, and not even that big if it's a new one. I look back out to the ocean but I can't see the parent bird. Where did it go? Has it lost its mate? Is there more than one eaglet?

I wait quietly for a few minutes, and then sure enough, I see the parent eagle light on the limb of a cedar tree in the distance and begin calling over and over again out to sea. It sounds heartbroken. Something must have happened to its mate.

I spot the remnants of an old swing in the fir beside me. The tire is long gone, but the knotted length of rope hangs only feet away from me. If I can shinny up fifteen feet or so, I can easily scale the trunk through the myriad of branches that begins a little way up. Before I can decide whether or not this is a good idea, my thongs are off my feet and I am already half way up the rope. Climbing is something I do well, probably a result of spending so many summers up Mt. Maxwell on Salt Spring. In my group of friends, if you can't climb a tree, you don't make the cut.

When I reach the first knot of branches where the rope is tied, I take hold of a nearby limb and hoist myself up. When I hear those chicks, I feel a surge of adrenaline. I stand up slowly, making sure my feet are secure before I push my head through the screen of fir needles ahead. Branches crisscross in front of me, and getting through the spaces between them is no easy task. But I take it slow. High and higher, foot by foot. Soon my legs are scratched up but it isn't long before I can see the nest. The underside of it is just a few feet away. Piece of cake. I turn my head right and then left, carefully choosing my footing as I opt for the right, because the limbs look stronger.

I test each new foothold before I allow my full weight to rest on it. My mom would go ballistic if she saw this, but Amelia would be standing below, cheering me on. Amelia is my biggest fan.

I climb the last little bit quickly. There's no sign of life in Ramona's studio, but that could change in an instant. I take hold of the thickest part of the branch in front of me, and bringing my elbows close to my sides, hoist myself through the greenery until my foot finds another branch to rest on. I feel like a pretzel, but I don't dare move because now I have a clear view of the whole nest! It's not that big, so it must be a new one. It's a mess of twigs, and the inside is lined with thick greenery, a nature-made carpet.

I hold myself steady, holding my breath, and stare at the sight in front of me. I've never seen anything this cool before. There are two chicks, both of them dark brown with flecks of white here and there, and, thanks to my cousin Victor's shared knowledge of eagles, I'd say about eight weeks old. One is bigger than the other, but both of them look kind of freaked out to see me. The bigger one holds its wings protectively over something in the nest, and I look down near its feet to see what looks like (and smells like!) a gnarly piece of fish.

The other eaglet hangs back with his wings slightly out-stretched and his beak open, as though he's panting. He doesn't take his eyes off me. Neither of the chicks has the yellow eyes of their parents yet, or, in this case, *parent*. Instead, their eyes are dark, almost the same colour as their feathers.

I feel like I'm part of another world, suspended high in the tree, witnessing this from only feet away. I want to stay here forever, far from my mother and Ramona's constant chatter, just watching these little guys watch me. But I don't want to stress them out. I know first-hand what it's like to be stared at by strangers.

"See you, little dudes," I tell them, and begin to inch my way back down through the fir boughs. It's faster going down, but harder, and I catch my shirtsleeve on a broken twig and hear the fabric tear as I drop to a lower limb.

I'm halfway down when a full-grown eagle dive-bombs me from out of nowhere and my heart leaps into my throat! I am just past the big boughs and leaning out to reach for the rope for my final descent when it appears from behind and screeches past me so close I feel the wind from its wings on my forearm. I can't blame the eagle. It's just being a good parent.

"I'm sorry," I whisper when my feet are finally firmly planted on the ground. I pick up my thongs and run quickly across the grass to the tiny deck off my shed.

The eagle goes straight into the tree, to the nest, and when it's sure that no harm has come to its young, it lands on the grass near the kayaks. I'm pretty sure it's the male. He's not all that big. The females are always bigger, with longer beaks.

I watch as the good father hops up and down along the water's edge, occasionally stopping to investigate some hidden remnant of shell or random crab leg on the ground. There's something odd about the way he moves. Not the way he struts so much, but the pattern of steps he takes. He walks forward three steps, and then walks backward for two. At first I think he's just checking out some tasty morsel he missed the first time, but soon it becomes obvious that this is just what he does. Three steps forward, two steps back. Three forward, two back. Over and over again, up and down on the grass. It must take him forever to get anywhere on foot! I smile. *Two-Step*. The bird has a name.

When he trades beachcombing for flight and takes off, I pull out my sketchbook and technical pen from my duffle bag and make a quick sketch of the two chicks—the larger one with his prized piece of fish, and the smaller, more timid one that's more focused on me than his sibling's lunch.

When I hear Ramona return from shopping, I hold my drawing in front of me and study it. Considering I haven't drawn anything for weeks, it could be worse.

I look up from my sketchbook to see papa eagle coming across the narrows with a little fish in his talons. The flash of silver catches the sun, but when the eagle is almost at the shore, the fish comes loose and plummets straight into the water.

"Smooth move, Two-Step," I say under my breath. But then I realize the eagle isn't stupid. He's just tired.

Chapter Thirteen

❧

HANNAH

"LOOK OVER THERE!" I say suddenly, pointing to the back of the Salish Sea Studio where I'll soon be working. The quaint, bright-blue cottage sits tucked in beside the Old Rose Bed and Breakfast, and a grassy slope rolls down behind it to the water. There are two little cabins that sit along the wooden boardwalk leading from the house to the dock.

"Where?" Max hisses.

"Ramona's place. Just up from her kayaks. Look at those fir trees." Max follows my finger and his eyes widen.

"I see it! It's a bald eagle for sure."

There's no mistaking that bright white head. It's sitting at the top of a stand of trees just up from the shore, and now that we can see it, we can hear it, too. Faint little "screes" at evenly spaced intervals—funny twittering noises.

"I wish your mom were here," I tell Max. "She'd know what it was trying to say."

"Do you see a nest?"

"No, do you?"

"No, but let's go over. Ramona won't mind." Max is already down the platform steps and starting to jog along the pathway. I match his pace, but I'm out of breath by the time we reach the edge of Trumpeter's Field. When we get to the gnarled, long-forgotten fruit trees, planted on the old farm that used to be here, we push our way through and run smack into a man holding a pair of binoculars.

"Oh!" I say, startled. "Sorry!"

He grunts at us. He's wearing a black-and-red-check flannel shirt, and a red ball cap pulled low over scraggly dark hair. He has one of those Fu Manchu moustaches, the kind that ends at the bottom of his chin. There is something oddly familiar about him. It takes me a second, but then I remember: the guy from the hardware store. The guy with the red truck! I think his name was Kelso.

I look at the ground near his feet and see a couple of empty Big Mountain beer cans, a potato chip bag, and two cigarette butts. And there's no mistaking that sickly, sweet smell that hangs heavy in the air around us. Pot.

This guy isn't your average Tilley-hat wearing birdwatcher.

I stare at the garbage on the ground and frown, but the guy just shrugs. "It's just the woods, kid." Then, to make his point, he kicks a beer can far into the bushes with his foot.

"Hey!" Max says, lunging for the can.

The man puts his binoculars into the pocket of his shirt, then faces me as he mashes the cap farther down on his head. "Well, that's enough sightseeing for one day. Have a nice day, kids. Stay outa trouble."

He walks across Trumpeter's Field to the parking lot and stops next to the red 4x4. We don't take our eyes off him as he leans against it, pulls out a phone, and begins texting.

"Are you thinking what I'm thinking?" I say to Max.

"That it's definitely the same truck we saw last night?" Max says with narrowed eyes.

"And the same one that was at the hardware store."

"I know," agrees Max.

I turn around and pick up the discarded beer cans and chip bag, stuffing them all into my backpack.

We watch the man put his phone in his pocket, climb in the truck, and head toward Duncan.

"The dude's obviously a total stoner," Max says.

"I think he's more than that."

We run the rest of the way to Salish Sea Studio, and by the time we get there, we hear the eagle loud and clear.

"Hey, Han. Look who wants in on the action," Max says, grinning as he points to an alder tree in Ramona's yard. There sits Jack, doing his usual manic-shuffling-hoppy dance to get my attention. He looks normal enough, but I'm not buying. I'm still recovering from the stunt he pulled at school.

"Hey, buddy," I say cautiously, peering up into the tree. "You'd better keep your distance if you know what's good for you." But I know that, despite what the books say, Jack is no threat to eaglets. He's more interested in old pizza crusts than baby raptors.

Jack ignores my advice and flaps down to light on my shoulder—something he doesn't do very often—and steadies himself by grabbing a piece of my hair with his beak.

"Ouch!" I yell. "Quit that!"

We start along the cobblestone pathway that leads from the road, down past the side of Ramona's cottage, and see a girl standing under the trees at the bottom of the slope. She's looking straight up, and she's holding a dead fish.

"Hello?" Max says, and the girl turns around. She looks from Max to me and then to Jack. Our eyes lock and my legs feel as though they're made of Jell-O. I think I might fall over as Jack steadies himself again on my shoulder. Her face! Those eyes!

The fish drops from the girl's hand and she steps backward into the tree, as surprised by us as we are by her. I can't stop staring. Max shoots me a look as though I've lost my mind, but even so, my eyes are glued on her. It's uncanny how much she looks . . .

I try to shift my feet but they remain immovable objects, firmly cemented in the grass. I should blink, or look away, or say something about what nice weather we're having, but I can't seem to break this Mexican standoff the girl and I are having. She is not very tall, shorter than me, maybe fifteen or sixteen, with short, punk-rockish, dark red hair. Her faded jeans are baggy and ride low on her hips, and the black t-shirt she's wearing has a big rip in one of the sleeves and a smear of fish guts down the front. But it's not her clothes or her hair. It's her face! The straight slope of her nose, the high cheekbones, the deep-set, intense black eyes, and especially the defiant way she juts her jaw out. I just can't believe it. The resemblance. It's—

"What's *with* you?" Max whispers, shoving me slightly and forcing my feet to "unstick." Jack jumps from my shoulder to the ground, where he begins walking toward the girl, or rather the fish that is now lying on the grass beside her. He's sort of pigeon-toed, and with his blue-black head bobbing from side to side as he picks his way forward, the effect is kind of funny. At any other time, I'd be laughing. But not today. Not right now.

"Hey!" The girl looks straight at Jack and then at me. I finally manage to find my voice and blurt out, "Oh, it's okay. Jack's just curious. He won't eat that fish if that's what you're worried about. He actually prefers bagels and muffins. I mean, he hangs out at the Toad in the Hole bakery a lot, you know?" I close my mouth, feeling like I've said way more than I need to. I always talk a lot when I'm feeling nervous.

"What did you call him?" The girl's eyes grow wide.

"Who? Jack?" I feel myself going red. "I know it's sort of stupid to call a—"

"He's your pet or something?" she interrupts.

If Jack could roll his eyes, I'm sure he would have. I swear he gets insulted when he hears the word "pet." But instead, he hops right over the fish and looks high up into the tangle of green boughs above our heads.

I look back to the girl, and I feel as though I am suddenly back in Tl'ulpalus, two years ago, on the trail where I met her for the first time.

Yisella. She looks *exactly* like Yisella.

Chapter Fourteen

※

IZZY

I'M NOT GOING TO LIE. Looking at this girl with the psycho red hair standing in front of me, and with that raven on her shoulder, well, it shakes me up. I know my mother's stories are completely bogus, but even still, the coincidence is creepy.

What makes it even weirder is the staring. I mean, people stare at me a lot, and not usually in an approving sort of way, but this girl doesn't seem focused on my punky hair or my clothes or my pierced eyebrow. She just stares at me in that "I've forgotten how to blink" kind of way. What choice do I have but to stare right back? She may or may not be a living legend, but no one wins a staring contest with Izzy Tate.

"I'm Max," the boy says, "and this is Hannah, and, I guess you've sort of met Jack."

The girl—Hannah—glares at him.

"We're looking for an eagle nest," Max explains. "A mature eagle was killed yesterday, and we think there might be eaglets in that tree."

Two-Step's mate? It has to be!

"There are," I say. "Two of them."

"You found them already?" Max looks up and takes a few steps toward the tree. "Are you sure?"

Just then, Ramona, back from her trip into the village, appears from the other side of the cottage, her bare feet peaking out from under her flowing yellow chiffon skirt. "Oh!" she says when she sees the three of us. "Hey, you guys. You startled me. I see you've met Isabelle Tate!"

"Actually, it's Izzy," I say. Only my mother calls me Isabelle.

The boy—Max—looks at me suspiciously, and then to Hannah, who is still staring. What is her problem, anyway? Talk about rude.

"Izzy is staying here for a few weeks," Ramona says. "She's going to be helping soon, in the studio this summer. Just like you, Hannah. Izzy's mom is a terrific knitter. Louise Tate? I bet you've heard of her. Anyway, I'm sure you two will get along famously."

Great. In addition to my soon-to-be fascinating summer job and five-star sleeping accommodation, I also get a new, bug-eyed best friend thrown into the mix. Yay.

Ramona smiles and picks up the front of her skirt, stepping carefully over the old railway ties that terrace the slope, most of which are covered by overgrown and unidentifiable herbs. "What are you guys looking at anyway?"

"Eagles," Hannah says. "We found a dead one on the road last night. It hit the power line. That's what caused the power outage at the marina."

"Where is it?" I demand.

"We don't know," Max says, looking confused. "We had to leave it where it was for a couple of minutes and when we got back, it was gone."

"What?"

"It was gone," Max repeats.

"What do you mean, it was gone?" I say, stiffening.

"Uh . . . like I just said. It was gone. No longer in the vicinity. G.O.N.E."

"Then someone must have taken it," I say, furious.

"Ya think?" There is a distinct note of sarcasm in Max's voice.

"Come on now, calm down, everyone. Can somebody please explain to me what's going on here?" Ramona gently touches my arm, speaking in her quiet, slowed-down "guidance-counsellor" voice. It's patronizing, and I shrug her hand away.

"An eagle was killed yesterday," Max says, "on the power lines."

"And now there's only one parent left to take care of the

chicks. And Izzy says there are two of them up there." Hannah points, and then shoves her hands in the back pockets of jeans that are at least an inch too short. Is *everybody* fashion-challenged in Cowichan Bay?

"Two?" Ramona says, sounding surprised. "How do you know?"

"I climbed the tree," I tell Ramona. But before she can have a coronary, I add, "Don't get all twisted about it. I climb trees all the time."

"You didn't!" Ramona says, covering her mouth with both hands while she looks up the tree. "All the way up there? For heaven's sake, Izzy! That wasn't a very smart thing to do while you were here by yourself. You could have fallen and broken your neck!"

"Well, I didn't."

"What did they look like?" Max asks, like an over-enthusiastic puppy. "Are they okay? Are they very old?"

"They're fine," I say.

"We should call someone to come get them," Max says, crossing his arms over his chest.

"NO!" I frown at him. Who suddenly made this guy the boss?

"Isabelle," Ramona soothes, "will you please just take a moment and calm down."

"Forget it, Ramona," I tell her. "I'm *not* going to calm down! People are always screwing around with animals like this, so don't pretend they aren't! I saw that article you circled in the paper, the one about the elk poaching. It was disgusting. So yeah, calming down isn't going to work for me, okay?" It's the most I've spoken since I arrived, and while Ramona probably didn't deserve my outburst, I'm too angry to care. I push past everyone, accidentally knocking Hannah's shoulder with my own as I run up to the cottage.

"Hey!" I hear her say.

"Yeah. What's your problem?" Max calls after me.

I storm into Ramona's kitchen, letting the screen door slam behind me, but not before I hear Ramona's soft voice. "Izzy is . . . Izzy has had a bit of a hard time, guys. Some family stuff. You know. She's not a bad kid. She's just, well—"

"A jerk?" Max says, and I flatten myself out beside the door so I can listen.

Ramona sighs. "I know she was out of line just then. But you have to understand her circumstances, not that I'm excusing her rudeness."

"Where does she live?" Hannah blurts out.

"Over on Salt Spring Island. But her mom and I thought it might do her some good to get away for a bit. And Cowichan Bay is where her mother's family is originally from."

"No way! She's Cowichan?" Hannah says this like I'm some kind of rare alien life form.

"Her mom is," I hear Ramona say. Of course there is no mention of my dad. "Anyway, cut her some slack, okay guys? Just give her a bit of time to settle in. She'll be fine."

I don't wait to hear anymore. I walk straight through the

house, out the front door, and then along the road that runs down to the village. Fish. The chicks will be hungry again in no time. I dig in my pocket and find a couple of crumpled five-dollar bills. I bite my lower lip. Looks like I'm either buying fish or buying smokes because I can't afford both. But I see Two-Step in my mind: hear his frantic calls, remember his dropped dinner, and the tired way he walked on the ground. I take a deep breath, smooth out the bills, and head toward the fish market.

❈

On my way back to Ramona's, I stop briefly by one of the picnic tables near the ocean to remove a stone from inside my shoe. I find it, and throw it toward the beach. The water is calm and quiet. There's nothing moving out there except a flock of pigeons flying past to settle on some crappy-looking ship out in the bay.

"Hey," someone says. I look up and see a skinny blonde twenty-something guy, wearing jeans and a leather jacket, standing a few feet away. I don't answer him.

"You smoke pot?" he asks, taking off the jacket. He has a tattoo up his forearm. Two words: *Wake & Bake.* How original.

"No thanks," I tell him.

"Ha. Bet you do. I can assure you it's good," he says. "Best on the island."

"Not interested."

He looks like he's about to sit down beside me, but thankfully doesn't. There is some blondish peach fuzz above his upper lip and he smells as though he just took a bath in a vat of cheap, drugstore aftershave. He rates a nine out of ten on my internal creep metre.

"Sure you won't change your mind?"

When I don't answer him, he shrugs. "Well, later, then. How about a couple of j's? Five bucks a joint. Sweet deal. It's Purple Haze, babe."

"I said I'm not interested."

"Okay, your loss. Just means more for me." He smiles, revealing a row of stained yellow teeth. "Name's Buzz, and I sure hope I see you around. I'm a fool for a pretty girl." He ambles slowly up to the road, head down, texting as he goes. Minutes later, a guy with a lame '70s mustache driving a red 4x4, stops near the entrance to the parking lot, picks him up, and drives away.

So far, I'm not too impressed with Cowichan Bay.

Chapter Fifteen

HANNAH

DAD'S AT HIS WRITER'S group meeting when I get home, so I fix myself some baked beans on toast for dinner.

Poos isn't a fan of beans and stays asleep on top of the microwave in the kitchen, but Chuck follows me to the armchair in the living room, taking swipes at my feet. My guess is he's hoping I have improved my sharing skills since the last time I ate in front of him. Sorry, Fatso. Drama makes me hungry.

When I finish the last of the toast crusts, I grab my diary from the window ledge where I left it for anyone to read (*dumb!*) and open it on my lap. I keep it brief, not like the entries I used to make when I was younger. I remember one of Dad's Golden Rules of Writing: Don't use ten words when you can use two. It's a pretty good rule.

After I finish, I shut the cover and make a note-to-self to be a little more diligent about my privacy. It's not like my diary is future movie material, but still . . . there are some things that are meant only for my eyes.

I run up the stairs to my loft, planning to hide it under the bed, behind a box of long-forgotten stuffed animals. It's where I keep all my old diaries, although the one I just finished a week ago is still hiding out in my sock drawer. I dig around for it and pat the cover. "Too risky," I tell it. "You belong under the bed, too."

I crouch down to pull out the rolling box of stuffies, followed by my journals in the cloth shopping bag. But there are only two inside. There should be three. And the one that's missing is *that* diary—the blue one with the golden sun faces splashed across the cover—the one I wrote the summer I was twelve. How I'd spent so much time documenting everything I could remember from that trip back through time to T'lulpalus. Every single detail so I would never forget.

I lie flat on the floor and shimmy under my bed, but other than a few oversized dust bunnies and a missing slipper, there is no blue diary. It's gone. I feel cold all over, and my pulse races.

Sabrina Webber! How else would she know about the summer of 2010? I clench and unclench my fists, racking my brain, trying to think how my diary might have found its way into her hands.

I spend the rest of the evening trying not to think about it, but end up thinking about nothing else. By nine o'clock I feel as though I'm about to crack up, so I grab my hoodie, stuff my feet into my sandals, and head out the door. Dad's writer's group doesn't usually end until midnight, so I don't bother to leave him a note.

As soon as I'm outside, I smell cinnamon and apples and sugar and all things wonderful. It can mean only one thing. Nell, who doesn't keep regular baker's hours, is making her famous danishes.

"Hannah Banana! I made danishes!" Nell calls out when I see her at the back door of the Toad in the Hole as I walk up Dock #5. I cringe only for a second at the "banana" part because tonight I'm way beyond being bothered by that dumb childhood moniker. I raise my hand in a wave and jog up the walk to her shop.

There are trays of danishes a mile high inside the bakery's kitchen, just waiting to be glazed. It's perfect. I need a nice mindless task, and I know Nell will let me do it. She's cool like that, and she's also psychic.

"What's wrong, Han?" she asks before I'm even in the door. "Something bugging you?"

"Kind of." I take a stool by the counter along the back window, and look out at the boats twinkling on the water. I look at the *Orca I*. Nothing. No lights. No little orange boat. No shadowy figures. The bay is flat calm tonight. Still and quiet.

"Well," Nell says, pointing to a tray on the counter, "feel free to sample one. I've just got a couple of touchy things in the ovens right now. Back in a jiff." She places a fourth tray down on the wire rack at the end of the counter and brushes some hair out of her face. As usual, she's a mess; there's flour across one eyebrow and a big fruity stain on her shirtsleeve. Ironically, her apron is spotless.

"Thanks, Nell." I roll up my sleeves and then reach for a warm danish.

"I'm firing up the java!" Ben bursts through the front door, talking to no one in particular. He hangs out at the bakery after hours a lot. Nell says he just likes to be helpful, but I'm pretty convinced he has a giant crush on her. He always shows up in a good shirt and that's a clear sign if you ask me.

They should bottle bakery smells and call it *Eau de Délices* or something similar. I don't want to be any place else but here right now. This place is so familiar to me. It's comforting.

When I was little, I used to colour at the counter by the window, using big, chunky crayons that Nell still keeps in a china jug on the shelf beside the ancient retsina wine bottles. I've even stayed over, helping Nell pull all-night baking marathons when she had a wedding order or something.

When the coffee maker starts to gurgle, Ben walks over to the vintage radio by the cash register and fiddles with the knobs until he settles on Classic Country 107.3.

"Oh, please Ben, no!" Nell calls from the kitchen. "Do we have to listen to country even at this late hour?"

"No better time," he says, cranking the volume.

"That stuff will rot your brain. Nothing but dying dogs and old trucks and cheatin' hearts," Nell sings.

But Ben is unfazed, and when Nell reappears with a pained expression on her face, Ben swoops in, grabs her and begins waltzing her around in circles on the floor.

"Let go of me, you crazy old man," she laughs, but he doesn't. Instead he dips her and spins her around and sings along with Hank Williams Sr. at the top of his lungs:

Hey, Good Lookin', whatcha been cookin'?
How's about cookin' somethin' up with me?

For an old guy, he's pretty light on his feet. I laugh out loud because, really? Chilling with Nell and Ben and a warm apple danish is not a bad way to end a weird day. I guess things could be a whole lot worse.

An hour later when I leave the bakery, I feel infinitely better. There's nothing like a little sugar therapy to restore a person's peace of mind.

I jump from the dock up onto our deck, and am about to give the sweet peas a drink from the rain barrel when Jack appears, soaring silently over my head. He swoops down low and, sure enough, delivers yet another "gift" for me. My breath catches in my throat as the object pings off a deck chair, bounces off the side of the cedar planter, then comes to rest inches away from my feet. I turn on the porch light and a shiver runs down my back.

Lying directly in front of my left foot is a large yellow claw. A perfectly shaped, neatly severed, eagle talon.

Chapter Sixteen

"DO YOU LIKE IT THERE, IZZY? Do you have to eat broccoli?" Amelia asks me this when I finally call home to say hi. Dinner was a cheese sandwich and some apple slices. Not exactly gourmet, but it seemed like a better alternative to Ramona's falafel kabobs. ("Feel Awful" kabobs, if you ask me.)

"No broccoli, Amelia," I tell her, smiling. I can imagine her round face at the other end of the phone, her earnest eyes all wide and innocent. "But you know what?"

"What?" she asks, breathless.

"I climbed a big tree a few days ago, and know what I found?"

"Don't tell! Let me guess!"

It's a game we've played ever since she could talk. When I say, "Guess what?" Amelia always guesses. She'll go on forever, but eventually I have to stop her and get on with the story.

"A big kite?" she asks.

"Nope. Not even close."

"Um . . . a magic apple?" Such an imagination.

"No," I tell her. "Apples come in the fall. You know that."

"What about a snake? One of those fat boa connectors that swallow people?"

I laugh. "Boa *constrictors*! Nope. Want me to tell?"

"NO!" she protests. "Let me guess!"

"Okay. Just one more though. This is long distance, remember?"

"Okay, okay," she sulks, and then perks up to say, "I know! You found a talking owl who granted you three wishes!"

I walk out to the front porch and sit in the wicker chair. "Now that *would* be a great find!" Three wishes. Imagine!

Ramona is on her hands and knees in the front garden, pulling weeds and tossing them one by one into the red bucket beside her.

"I would wish for pink ballet shoes, a horse named Taffy, and all the candy in the world!" Amelia shouts into the phone.

"Good wishes," I tell her, "but I didn't find an owl. I found some baby eagles."

"Baby eagles? Really?" Amelia says solemnly, her voice quiet again. "Like the kind we saw at Victor's house? The kind with the fuzzy white stuff all over them?"

"Nah. These ones are a little older. They're mostly dark brown. I wish you could see them, Amelia. They're so cool. One of them is bigger than the other, and I think the smaller one is kind of shy. He didn't move around much in the nest. Just kind of stayed behind his brother and watched me."

"He sounds like Oscar!" Amelia says. Oscar is her friend in kindergarten who always sits on the bench at recess, watching the other kids play on the monkey bars, but never joining in.

"You know," I say, "he is *exactly* like Oscar."

"Well . . ." Amelia says. I can hear her crunching on something as she talks. A carrot, most likely. Amelia is always eating carrots. I tease her that she's part rabbit. "Then that should be his name. Oscar. What's the other one like?"

"Mmmmm . . . he has a very good appetite. He eats everything I bring him so fast! And he's also pretty fancy on his feet."

Amelia loved this. "A fancy dancer! You should give him a dancing name!"

"A dancing name?"

"Yeah. What's that fancy dance you do when you stick a rose in your teeth? I saw a man and a lady doing it on TV and the lady was wearing bright red lipstick and was biting onto a rose."

"Oh," I say. "The tango."

"Yeah! The tango! That should be his name!" Amelia squeaks.

"Tango, it is. Oscar and Tango."

"Izzy?" Amelia stops crunching her carrot.

"Uh huh?"

"I miss you. It's hard to go to sleep because you aren't here to read me stories like you usually do."

"Won't Mom read to you?"

"She's really busy. She said she would yesterday but I think she forgot."

My heart twists up and my cheeks grow hot. It's so typical of Mom. If she wasn't so busy helping other people and their families, she might have ten minutes now and then for her own.

"Hey," I say, "I know most of your favourite books off by heart. Want me to do Grandma Lucille?"

"YAY!" Amelia shrieks.

Grandma Lucille is about a crazy old lady who rides a motorcycle and lives in a tree fort with a pet rat named Monty. It's one of Amelia's favourites. It would be nice if adults like "Grandma Lucille" existed in the real world, but who am I kidding? People get more stoked about cleaning gutters and mowing lawns than they do about building tree forts or taming rats.

After I say goodnight to Amelia, Ramona looks up from her weeding and smiles from across the grass. There are little insects buzzing all around her, backlit from the sun that's setting in the distance. They form a kind of pulsing golden halo around her head. She straightens up on her knees and places both hands on the small of her back.

"Ooooh," she says, "my bones are feeling their age tonight."

"Why do you bother pulling weeds then?" I ask.

"Hah," she says, giving me a wink. "If you just sit around and let the nasty stuff take over, the good stuff can't get through."

Another metaphor for life, compliments of Ramona.

But I get up from the chair and begin pulling weeds near the driveway.

Chapter Seventeen

❦

HANNAH

"MORE COFFEE, DAVID?" Beatrice asks my dad. We're sitting in the corner of the Salty Dog Café, enjoying our usual: a basket of prawns for Dad and fish and chips for me. We do this a couple of times a month because Dad says a little routine in our lives is a good thing. I'm fine with routine, especially when it involves halibut and tartar sauce.

"Thanks, Bea," he says as she refills his cup. Coffee number three, not that I'm counting.

"So," I say after she's gone, "do you think that talon Jack brought me is related to the poaching that's going on?"

"Could be," Dad says, looking out at the boats in the ma-

rina. "That talon was cut. Cuts like that don't occur naturally."
He's right. It was severed clean.

I want to tell him about the other stuff, but I'm not stupid.
The last thing I need is for him to go all "concerned-parent"
on me and cancel his trip to Spain. He needs to get away in
the worst way.

"About your bird friend," Dad says. "Don't ravens like to
collect things? Aren't they sort of famous for that?"

But I'm suddenly struck dumb. Not because I have nothing to say about ravens, but because I'm horrified to see Mrs.
Webber, Sabrina, and her uncle Ray—the man in the black
Hummer—come through the door of the restaurant. He looks
out of place in the Salty Dog, wearing an expensive looking
pair of slacks, a crisp white shirt, and shiny black leather
loafers. The smell of his cologne overtakes the usual one of
fish and chips that always hangs in the air.

"Oh no," I whisper, slumping lower in my chair.

"What's the matter?" Dad asks, reaching for the hot chili
sauce.

"Toxic waste alert at three o'clock." I grab the laminated
menu from behind the sugar dispenser on the table and open
it up in front of my face. I'm torn between wanting to hide
and wanting to lob the lemon slices from my plate at Sabrina's
head. Diary stealer!

Too late.

"Hi Hannah," Sabrina and her mother say in identical,
sugar-coated voices.

I look up over my menu, trying to look bored. "Oh. Hello." Sabrina is wearing a white tank top with the words *"BABY GUUURRRL"* looping across it in a swoopy, cursive font the same shade of blue as her thickly applied eyeshadow. I think there is glitter involved, in the letters *and* in the eyeshadow.

"Having fish and chips?" she singsongs.

No, I'm having Spider Monkey feet and bamboo worms. What does it look like?

To my horror, Dad gestures to the empty end of the table with its two unoccupied chairs. "You guys care to join us? I'm sure we could snag a couple more chairs from Bea."

I can't believe it. For a smart guy, my dad can be incredibly dumb sometimes. But to my relief Sabrina says, "Oh, thanks, Mr. Anderson, but we've got a table reserved already, two over from you guys."

"But thank you just the same," Mrs. Webber says. She has a stoic smile stretched across her face, revealing two rows of straight and unnaturally white teeth. "Ray?" she says, turning to Sabrina's uncle, "Reenie goes to school with Hannah here. And this is Hannah's father, David Anderson. He's a famous author, you know."

"Hah!" Dad laughs. "Famous! In my next life, perhaps."

The well-dressed man thrusts his hand out to my father. "Great to meet you, David! I'm Ray Webber. You sure are lucky to live in this piece of paradise I have to say! God's country, isn't it?" He shakes my dad's hand vigorously and then slaps a business card down on the table.

"No complaints here," Dad says, nodding. "You from out of town?"

"Mainland, originally," Ray Webber says. His smile is a lot like Sabrina's mom's: big, and too white. "I'm over here on business. I'm in boat salvage."

"Really?" Dad says.

"Got the contract a while back to haul that old wreck in the bay away. The *Orca I*."

"You don't say?" Dad wipes a little chili sauce from the corner of his mouth.

"Although," Ray says, smiling, "a buddy of mine managed to turn over that old engine the other day. Had her running pretty good. Not dead yet. Maybe she's got a few good years left in her still."

My father is clearly impressed. "Well, maybe she does and maybe she doesn't. Either way, I can't say I'm going to miss that ship. A lot of people are sure going to be happy to see it go."

"You can say that again," Bea says, coming up beside the Webbers with a pot of coffee in her hand. "That thing is an environmental disaster."

"Oh, don't you worry about that," Ray Webber laughs. "I've got it *all* covered. I'll give you guys back your bay, nice 'n' pretty the way it ought to be. And, I might add, the way it ought to stay!"

Bea laughs and flutters her free hand in front of her face, and a few people sitting at the surrounding tables start to cheer. My dad's smile is almost as big as Ray Webber's, but I hold back with my own. There's something about him that rubs me the wrong way. Maybe it's the big diamond pinky ring he's wearing on his right hand. Maybe it's his too-white teeth. Or maybe he's just too friendly.

"Well, aren't you folks just about the friendliest people I've ever met!" Ray says, laughing. "That's quite a welcome. I say drinks for everyone. On me!"

"Oh no, Mr. Webber!" Bea says incredulously. "We've got a full house tonight."

"No, no. I insist, Mrs. Lawson!" Ray says.

"Oh, call me Bea." Bea is clearly flustered. I think she's even blushing.

Ray puts an arm around her shoulder. "And you can call me, Ray."

"Well," Sabrina says, "I don't know about anyone else, but I'm dying for a big, yummy green salad!" She puts her hands on her narrow waist and smiles at her mother who pokes her in the ribs.

"That's my girl!" Mrs. Webber says. "Salads and soda water. That's how we Webber women stay so skinny!"

I spear about nine thousand french fries on the fork and stuff them into my mouth with an exaggerated flourish of my wrist.

"Goodness!" Mrs. Webber says, pushing a strand of honey-streaked hair out of her eyes. "French fries! And so many! You're certainly brave, Hannah!"

"Oh my God." Sabrina says, looking disgusted. "Ew."

I smile and chew, not caring that there is ketchup on my chin.

"Well, I'm sure you'll feel differently about those deep-fried little devils when your body starts to develop, honey," Mrs. Webber says, and I stop chewing like someone just flipped off a power switch. She did *not* just say that. Did she? I look over to Dad who is smiling the smile of the ignorant, happily consuming his breaded prawns from the basket in front of him.

Sabrina gives me a little pity-smile and adds, "Oh, it's *so* true, Hannah. When you *eventually* get boobs and stuff, you'll gain weight just by THINKING about french fries. I haven't been able to touch junk food like that for ages!"

"Thanks for the heads up," I say, sweetly. "I'll be sure to make a note about that in my *diary*." Sabrina doesn't bat an eyelash at the word, and even though I have lost my appetite, I keep stuffing the fries into my mouth on principle.

"Is Max working tonight?" Sabrina says, flipping her hair dramatically over her shoulder while she scans the restaurant.

Like I'm going to talk about Max with you!

So I don't tell her that Max and I have a kayak date later on when the sun goes down. Instead I just stare at her and chew.

"Sabrina? Alexis?" Ray Webber interrupts. "Let's leave these fine folks to their dinner and find our table, shall we?"

Sabrina and Mrs. Webber say goodbye, and walk over to their table, which, in my opinion, is nowhere near far enough away. I can still smell the sickly sweet floral perfume that Sabrina's mom is wearing, mixed in with her uncle's potent aftershave.

I put my fork down at the side of my plate and sneak a peak at my chest. Jeez. While I'm not exactly Pamela Anderson, it's plainly obvious that I'm a girl!

But I am distracted a moment later by a red truck that pulls up in the parking lot and parks next to Ray Webber's Hummer.

It's him! Kelso: the guy from the hardware store and Trumpeter's Field. I watch him open the back of the Hummer, and add a large box to a bunch of other ones that are stacked in the back. I see the words "Buddy's Hydroponics" written across several of them. Kelso throws a blanket over everything, slams the hatch shut and walks over to the Salty Dog, hesitating just inside the door of the restaurant for a moment while he talks on his phone. A moment later he walks over to join Sabrina's table. What? Why is he with them? And what's with the hydroponics stuff? People only use a ton of stuff from those stores for one thing: pot.

I wait until he looks up from his menu and then I glare at him with my best *you-can't-fool-me-I-know-you're-a-scum-bag-you-eagle-thief* look and I'm pretty sure he recognizes me, too, by the shifty way he sneaks a look at me for a nano-second.

Beatrice swoops in and mops up a coffee dribble near the edge of the table with a corner of her apron. "So," she says in a whisper, leaning forward a little, "how about that Ray Webber!"

Dad says, "Seems like a decent fellow."

"I wonder when he's going to move the boat out of the

bay? Did you notice his clothes? He must have pretty deep pockets. Those shoes are Italian leather." Bea sneaks a glance over to Sabrina's table at the same time that my dad picks up the business card beside his plate and turns around. Sabrina gives them a little wave. I nudge my dad with my foot under the table. Hard.

"Dad!" I mouth. "Don't!"

"Ouch! Don't what?"

"Could we please have some pie, Beatrice?" I ask politely,

"Oh, sure, Han. Blueberry, pecan or peach cobbler?"

"Um. Peach for me, please. With ice cream, too, maybe?"

"You got it. What about you, David?" Beatrice says, adjusting a bobby pin in her wiry grey hair.

"Same as always, Bea. Pecan please, 'cause I'm a bit of a nut."

In no time at all Beatrice places generous slices of her legendary homemade pies in front of us. As I lift a forkful of peachy awesomeness and vanilla ice cream to my lips, I notice Sabrina watching me with narrowed eyes as she chews on a piece of lettuce. I take another bite, just for her benefit, this one more ice cream than pie. Hey, if pie is off-limits to the Webber women, then they'll just have to live vicariously through me. The way I see it, I'm performing a random act of kindness: my good deed for the day.

Dad and I spend the next hour jabbering on about his upcoming trip to Spain. About how he still needs to buy good walking shoes and a decent daypack and that maybe it would be a good idea if he finally got an iPhone or a Blackberry for the camera and video features alone. We are deep in conversation about blisters and moleskin bandages, so we don't immediately hear the discussion at the cash register, not until we hear raised voices.

"Excuse me, Mr. Webber. But with all due respect you've had that contract for weeks now and I've yet to see any movement out in the bay." It's Riley, who eats at the Dog at least twice a week. He leans forward, shaking a bony finger right in front of Ray Webber's face. Dad looks at me with a raised eyebrow because Riley is normally a pretty quiet guy. He isn't one to make a scene. Usually he just holes up at a back table with his clam chowder and the newspaper.

"Ease up," Ray says, smirking. Unlike Riley, he looks cool as a cucumber.

"No!" Riley spits. "It's bad enough they didn't give the salvage contract to one of our local boys—Stanhope brothers would have had that tub out of here in a flash—but you got it and you aren't doing a damn thing with it! Why don't you pack up that gas guzzler of yours and head back to the city?"

"Hey, hey, settle down now. You just don't have all the facts, sir." Ray slouches sideways against the counter where the pies are displayed, and jingles a big ring of keys in his right hand. He makes a point of speaking to the pie case, instead of to Riley, which I decide is kind of rude. "You can't haul her out of the bay just like that. There are evaluations that need to be done first. Environmental impact studies, things like that. It takes time, my friend. It takes time."

"I'm not your friend," Riley says, leaning forward a little.

Kelso, the man with the red hat, gets up from the table and mutters something to Ray on his way out of the restaurant. Through the window, I see him lean against his truck and begin texting on his phone. (And they say teenagers have unhealthy attachments to their phones!)

Art comes through the swinging kitchen doors looking crankier than he normally does, which is saying something. "Is there a problem here, gentlemen?"

"All I know is that I smell a rat!" Riley steps forward so his face is only inches from Ray's. There is silence in the restaurant. A family coming through the door stops awkwardly, and then walks back outside again.

"This ends right here. Right now!" Art says, his voice strained and tight. There is a vein bulging out on one of his temples, and Beatrice, at the other end of the counter, is red-faced and wringing her hands together in her apron.

"Aw, hell. I'm sorry, Arthur," Riley says, "but I got a bad feelin' about this guy. He comes pushing his way into the village with his fancy car and clothes, thinking he owns the place. I just got a bad feeling in my gut."

I remember my conversation with Ben on the dock: *"Don't laugh, Hannah. Riley's gut is always right."*

"Riley?" Art says, his voice changing back from uptight to just plain cranky again. "Maybe it's time you went back to the *Tzinquaw,* huh? Take a load off. Look. Here. Take home some of Bea's peach pie." Art takes a plastic Tupperware container from Beatrice, and hands it over to Riley.

"You can't fix everything with a little dessert, Art," Riley tells him gruffly, but I can tell he's softening a bit, because his shoulders aren't pushed up into his neck anymore.

"True," Art agrees, "but it's still a damn fine piece of free pie, and you're a bigger fool than I thought if you walk away without it."

Riley takes the pie from Art and slaps him on the side of the arm, and then reaches over to rest his hand on Beatrice's shoulder. "Sorry, Bea. I was outa line."

"Go on," Art jokes. "Get out of here before I'm picking your teeth up off the floor . . . and cut your hair, ya damn hippie!"

Riley pushes out of the door, but not before turning to glare at Ray Webber, who is still leaning against the pie counter, and still spinning his keys on his finger.

"My apologies," Ray says to Bea and Art after the door closes. "I'm sure he was just concerned about the bay. I understand that, but I am sorry for the drama."

"Ah, forget it," Art says, extending his hand. The two men shake and slap each other on the back. "Riley's a little rough around the edges," Art laughs. I stifle a smile, because this is something, coming from Art!

Ray pays the bill while Sabrina and her mom skitter off to the ladies room. I watch carefully as Ray walks out to his Hummer, where Kelso shows him a message on his phone. Whatever it says doesn't sit well with him. He starts frowning and waving his arms around, and then points at the back of the Hummer. That perfect smile he was flashing around a little while ago is history.

Kelso gets into the 4x4 and peels out of the parking lot, just missing Quincy, who is lying in the evening sun near a planter box of petunias.

When Dad pays for our dinner and talks to Art, I pick up the business card from the table, absentmindedly making little tears in the edge so I don't have to look at Sabrina and her mother as they emerge from the washroom. That's when I notice the card says "Poseidon Salvage Inc." on the front. I've seen that before. I reach into my back pocket and unfold the card we found with the garbage in the woods. It's the same card. I put them both back into my pocket, and make a mental note to tell Max.

Dad motions from the cash register that we're good to go, but before I can get up, Sabrina and her mother clatter past me in their noisy, heeled sandals. They push past Beatrice without so much as a thank-you, and as the door closes behind them, I hear Sabrina say too loud, "Who puts raw mushrooms and beets in a salad anyway? Gross."

Aunt Maddie says you can tell a lot about people by the way they treat their waitress.

Chapter Eighteen

"PEACEFUL OUT HERE, ISN'T IT?" Ramona says. We are sitting at the end of her dock, having a late supper.

"It is pretty nice," I say. And it is. The wood is warm and smooth against our bare legs, and I can smell the honeysuckle that grows wild next door at the Old Rose Bed & Breakfast.

"Well," Ramona says, reaching for another piece of focaccia bread, "if you don't dig in soon, I'm going to have to eat all this by myself." She swirls a chunk of bread around in a shallow dish of olive oil and balsamic vinegar, pops it into her mouth and leans back in an old Adirondack chair, once bright red, but now mostly bare, sun-bleached wood.

"Is that yours?" I ask, pointing to a black kayak that's tethered to a post at the side of the dock.

"Yep." Ramona says. "Yep. She's kind of old, but she goes. Sort of like me." She laughs at her own joke, and doesn't seem to care that I don't.

"Would it be okay if I took it out sometime?"

"You know how to paddle?"

"I'm part Indian," I tell her. "Duh."

"Kind of a sweeping generalization, don't you think?" Ramona says, smiling.

"Maybe." I smile. "But I do know how to kayak."

"Well, in that case, be my guest."

"Thanks."

"Just one rule."

"What's that?"

Here we go.

"No one takes the *Black Swan* out unless they're wearing a life jacket." Ramona leans forward in the chair and gives me the hairy eyeball. "End of story."

"The *Black Swan*?"

"I saw one once, in Trumpeter's Field. Jet black. She was beautiful. I know, I know. I'm such a romantic. But my point is, life jackets are mandatory."

I look at the kayak's smooth, glossy black finish, and right away my fingers begin to itch. It would make an awesome canvas, and I haven't painted in such a long time.

"I don't suppose you'd let me doodle on it, would you?" I ask Ramona.

Without hesitation, she says, "Are you kidding? Go crazy!

Paint anything you like here, Izzy. You know I'm a big art fan."

I nod a thank you. I have to hand it to her—she may be disorganized, have zero fashion sense and talk too much, but she is pretty chill when it comes to creativity. I decide to make some preliminary drawings later on in my sketchbook. Maybe I can play with the kayak's name, *Black Swan*, and work in some fine white line work, abstracted feathers and rippling water.

I turn my eyes from the kayak to the trees. Oscar and Tango are finally quiet, their bellies full of fish. Two-Step seems happy to let me help out with meals, but I know that what little cash I have isn't going to last very long if I'm the one doing the bulk of his grocery shopping. Still, it's awesome to watch Two-Step inch closer and closer to whatever I leave for him at the base of the tree. Three steps forward, two steps back. Three forward, two back, until finally he gets there. I'm getting used to smelling like fish.

There's a guy named Riley—a dude who has a fish boat called *Tzinquaw* in the marina. He gave me a pretty good deal on some salmon today. I'll have to visit him again. He seems pretty chill.

"Nice job with those eaglets, Izzy," Ramona says, looking up, "but maybe we should call the Raptor Centre tomorrow. You know, for advice."

"We don't need to," I tell her. "I can look after them myself. I've been doing it ever since I got here."

"Izzy—" Ramona begins, but I cut her off.

"It's really not a big deal, Ramona. Victor says that you just have to keep the food supply going until they're ready to feed themselves. Chances are they were born in May, so they won't be ready to fledge for another few weeks. I can help out for that long. Really, it's no trouble. I want to."

"Well. Okay, then," Ramona says, smiling. "It's great to see you so excited about something."

I change the subject before she goes off on a tangent. "The pasta salad was really good."

"Oh? Glad you liked it. There's lots left over so help yourself whenever you like."

We collect the plates and bring them back up to the kitchen. I scrape the scraps into the compost bucket under the sink, while Ramona goes out to feed Paco and Luna.

When I'm done in the kitchen, I flop down in the wicker chair on the porch, and flip absentmindedly through one of several gardening magazines. My eyes come to rest on an ad for gardening clogs. A woman in a bright purple t-shirt and hiking shorts is pushing a shiny wheelbarrow full of perennials across a perfectly mowed lawn. On her head is a green bandana, and on her feet, a pair of neon-green gardening clogs. She looks like some kind of radioactive garden gnome. Crocs should be illegal, for the ugly factor alone.

"I think I'm going to flop on my bed with a book," Ramona announces when she appears at the screen door. "You need anything before I turn in?"

"No thanks," I say. "I'm good."

"Okay. You know where to find me if you need me."

I nod, feigning interest in an article about worm composting until I'm sure that she has settled into her room for the night. I have to admit that she's actually not that awful. She sort of leaves me alone, doesn't push me to talk, and while there are things I really miss about Salt Spring, my mother's constant attempts to engage me in meaningful conversation at every waking moment is not one of them. She's never really embraced the "Silence is Golden" thing.

When the sun sinks lower and the house is quiet, I go to my cabin and change into a pair of jeans and a long-sleeved, zip-up hoodie. It's certain to be cooler out on the water. I put on my running shoes and sit on the bed to lace them up. There are a couple of framed photographs on the wall that I hadn't noticed before. One of Paco and Luna, both of them with brightly coloured South American blankets draped over their backs, and the other is a shot of Ramona and my mom when they were probably not much older than I am now. Mom is wearing hip-waders and a pink bandana over her hair. She's holding up a huge fish, making it look as though it's about to take a big bite out of Ramona, who is pretending to look terrified. I have to smile, because, well, it's kind of an awesome photograph.

❧

The evening sun fades into twilight and I watch the beads of water spill over my paddle as I dip it in and out of the water.

I haven't kayaked for a while, not since I tagged along on a camping trip to Horne Lake with my friend Samantha and her family, but it's kind of like riding a bike, and I'm pretty good with the paddle if I say so myself. I'd forgotten how relaxing it is, and after a few minutes I stop paddling to listen to the water and smoke one of the few cigarettes I have left. But the smoke overwhelms the smell of the saltwater and the fresh evening air, and after only two puffs I flick the end off into the water, butt it out and put it away to have later.

I glide along, parallel to the shoreline, and head toward the marina. When I see the docks running between the brightly coloured houseboats, I venture in a little closer. Some of the homes are tall and skinny, while others are single-storey, rustic cabin-like structures with wrap-around decks. How cool would it be to live on the water all year? What happens when there's a storm? Do people get seasick in their living rooms when the weather is rough?

I watch a couple of cats on one of the houseboat decks, batting around a rolled up sock: a big orange tomcat and a smaller tabby with a diamond of white fur just above its nose. The orange one sees me and stops the game, choosing instead to watch my kayak.

I'm thinking about paddling closer when two people, a man and a girl with wild red hair, jump from the dock onto the houseboat deck. It's her again! Hannah.

Not wanting to draw their attention, I slowly encourage the kayak to the right until I'm hidden behind a scuffed-up powerboat called *Sea Witch*.

Hannah and the man are laughing about something, and the joke continues as they move around on their deck. The raven—Jack—appears out of nowhere and lands on a deck chair beside them, and I can't help gripping my paddle a little tighter to my chest. Whether I want to believe it or not, that is definitely no ordinary bird.

I watch Jack hop along beside Hannah and the man that I assume is her dad. The bird leaps from one chair to another like a well-trained dog. They don't pay much attention to him, except when I hear Hannah say, "Here you go, Jack. Saved you some french fries, you spoiled bird."

More laughing, and then they go inside, closing the door behind them. A moment later a little light goes on upstairs, casting a dull glow over the deck. Jack doesn't leave right away. He stays perched on the back of the chair, preening his feathers and making fast work of the fries Hannah left for him on the metal armrest.

I'm surprised to discover that I'm shaking, even though I'm not cold. I have not allowed myself to consider this: my mother's crazy story about the magic raven and the girl who visited Cowichan Bay—Tl'ulpalus, as it was called then—over 150 years ago. What if it's true? What if, after all this time, there actually *is* something to that story? I shake my head. My mother can still get to me, even out here on the water.

By the time I paddle away from the marina, I've pulled myself together. None of this stuff matters anyway. *Hannah or no Hannah. Jack or no Jack. It makes no difference to me.* I keep paddling until I'm out into the open water. My mind clears, and I focus on dipping to the left, then to the right, repeating the rhythm over and over until I feel an old familiar tug in my shoulders and my wrists. With every pull, I am farther and farther away. Away from my mother. Away from the talking. *Away*. Stroke. Dip. Stroke. Dip. Over and over until all I am thinking about is the water breaking against the bow of the kayak in front of me, and the cleansing, salty smell that fills my nostrils.

When a trickle of sweat runs down my back, and the sting becomes more intense in my biceps and shoulders, I stop paddling and look around. I've reached the briny water of the estuary, where the ocean meets the mouths of the Cowichan and Koksilah rivers. I am nowhere near where I thought I would be. But it's beautiful here. I rest the paddle across the cockpit rim in front of me, and stare up to the sky, where, according to my mother, our ancestors came from. That's the legend, anyway. *Stutsun* and *Syalutsa*, two dudes who supposedly "fell out of the sky" and were the first people here. I know, lame, right? Imagine if I bought into it all:

"*Izzy? Where are you from?*"

"*Why, I'm so glad you asked. I'm from up there. Lovely weather most of the time, but a bit breezy now and then.*"

I laugh out loud in the half-light, and feel my muscles twitch and then relax. From somewhere on the shore a frog croaks, and the occasional muffled clang of a ship's bell can be heard from the marina. I close my eyes and listen, thinking

I could stay in this tranquil pocket of water forever.

I awaken to the banging, and I'm not sure where I am. What happened to the estuary? Have I been drifting? How long was I asleep?

Another bang sounds from farther out in the bay. It's impossible to pinpoint the source. I hear it again, and then again, until the bangs come every second or so—a beat that sounds like wood on wood.

I turn around as far as I can in one direction, and then in the other but I can't see anything. While I was asleep, twilight slipped away into darkness, and now I am not only cold, but quite possibly lost as well. I pick up the paddle and point the kayak toward the noise.

When the voices start up, I hold my breath. Men's voices. Chanting voices. Then, yelling. The steady drum beat grows louder and more frantic.

What *is* that? I paddle vigorously following the sound, but a fog is rolling in and soon it and the noises are all around me. I can just make out the jagged forms of the cliffs on a big mountain in front of me, which seem close enough to touch.

I place the paddle on the cockpit rim, and cover my ears to muffle the banging noise as it gets louder and louder. The shouting voices are angry. Threatening.

Despite the thickening fog, I have to find the source of the noise before I completely lose my nerve. I slice into the water on my left, and send the kayak to the right in a fast, smooth turn. I travel more or less blindly into the blanket of fog, listening for any other sounds that might orient me. But I can't concentrate. I raise my hands to cover my ears against the deafening noise, which seems to be coming out of the fog itself.

Shut up! Shut up! Shut up!

The *Black Swan* bumps against something hard, and veers abruptly to the left, sending me lurching in the opposite direction. I smack my shoulder against something that feels like a brick wall, and the banging and chanting stops. All I hear now is the gentle sound of the water lapping against my kayak. Even the fog is thinning. What is going on? Who was shouting? Who was so angry? Was it some kind of warning? Were they trying to scare me away? Or was I dreaming . . . drifting while I slept, and I only just now woke up? Am I becoming as flakey as everyone else in Cowichan Bay?

I rub my shoulder, realizing that I smacked up against a boat, one longer than a city bus! I tilt my head back and reach out to touch the barnacle-covered steel in front of me. Yup, it's real. It's got to be that big, creepy ship that sits in the middle of the bay.

And that's when I see them. Just beyond the bow of the barge, two deep yellow kayaks, side-by-side, heading directly toward me. Without hesitating, I maneuver my own boat backwards with a few swift strokes of my paddle, and then twist and tuck in behind the stern of the rust bucket. I fumble against the barnacles, unable to find anything to grab onto, and drift helplessly until my kayak stops against the side of the hull once again.

"I know I saw a light on in there," a voice says. A girl's voice.

"So what? You said Sabrina's uncle is salvaging it, right?" This time it's a boy.

I stay small and hidden, trying to hear what they're saying now that the banging has stopped. They *must* have heard it, too. The whole of Cowichan Bay must have heard it. It was loud enough to wake the dead.

"I know I saw two people in a tender here," whispers the girl.

"So what?"

"But it was 4:30 in the morning. You don't think that's weird?"

"Hannah? Don't be so dramatic."

Hannah? I thought so. It's Hannah and Max.

"Shhhhhh!," Hannah whispers. "What if someone's up there? What if they're watching us right now!"

"Hey. You're the one who wanted to investigate, so you'd better suck it up and grow a backbone."

"Yeah, yeah. Blah, blah, blah. Come on, let's paddle around the back. And keep your voice down."

"Okay, but find a way to tell Jack to quit dive-bombing my kayak," Max says.

"I know," I hear Hannah say. "He needs bird Ritalin or something."

I push away from the hull and glide toward the bow on the starboard side of the boat as the others reach the stern from the port side.

Why do I have the feeling this isn't going to end well?

Chapter Nineteen

HANNAH

"DID YOU HEAR SOMETHING?" I ask Max when we reach the *Orca I*. I spent the entire paddle out here talking to Max about Kelso and the red truck, and Ray Webber in the restaurant scene with Riley, and the hydroponic equipment in the back of Ray's Hummer. But now that we're out here, this secret nighttime paddle feels more stupid than adventurous.

"Just now. I thought I heard a splash." I look up to the rusted rail of the deck above my head.

"Han," Max says sarcastically, "we're sitting on a large body of water. A splash would not be unusual to hear."

"Very funny," I tell him, but I'm not laughing. This rusted

tub of steel is giving off a seriously creepy vibe. I give my head a shake and start to take mental notes: things that make me suspicious.

"Check out the ladder," I whisper at Max, pointing to the steel rungs a few feet away that climb up the steel to the deck. "Notice anything?"

Max pulls in a little closer, but just shrugs. "Lotta bird crap."

"Yeah," I say, "but no barnacles." The horizontal rungs are smooth and barnacle-free, yet every other surface is covered with them. "Means the ladder gets used a lot."

"Good eye, Detective Anderson," Max whispers, and then pokes at something caught behind the ladder on the surface of the water with the end of his paddle. "Hey. What's this?" He lifts his paddle, and balances a soggy cardboard box precariously on the end of it, its top caved in.

I pull in close and click on my Maglite, shining it directly on the box, which is decorated with a dull green camo pattern. On the front of the box is a picture of an elaborate, binocular-like apparatus attached to a head strap of some sort, and the words *NIGHT TRACKER—Series Tactical G1 Night Vision Goggles* is written across one side.

"Hey," Max whispers again. "No way. These are the real deal. Military issue."

A sliver of moonlight highlights one side of his face, and not in a good way. The huge shadows cast under his eyes make him look like some kind of saltwater zombie.

I stare at the box. Why would someone salvaging a broken-down boat need night vision goggles? I shiver, even though

I'm not cold. Maybe this *was* a stupid idea. After all, we're just a couple of fourteen-year-olds. But before I can say anything, Max scoots ahead of me in his kayak, his eyes fixated on a spot above his head.

"Check that out," he whispers. He points to a spot on the hull where a pipe, tightly wrapped with insulation, protrudes from the centre of a tiny porthole.

"What is it?" I ask, coming closer.

"Exhaust pipe," Max whispers. "Bet there's a generator on board. Come up closer. Listen."

We tuck in tight to the hull, and sure enough, there is a faint hum coming from deep inside.

"That's a generator, all right," Max says.

"I don't see any lights up there," I say, peering up to the deck of the *Orca I*, trying to cut through the black. "Do you think anyone's on board?"

"Nah," Max says. "Not unless they swam out here."

"Come on," I say, suddenly unsettled. "Let's go." I push my kayak away from the boat with the end of my paddle, passing the *NO TRESPASSING! DANGER!* warning that is painted in big white letters across the mid-section of the hull, while Max follows.

"Already?" Max says. "You turning chicken?"

"Shut up, Max."

I feel a pang of guilt. Why am I being awful to Max? After all, I dragged him into this. I change the subject. "I'm sorry, Max. It's just that I know something is going on. I mean, those goggles. You don't wear night vision goggles unless you're trying not to be seen. And why is there a running generator on board? I have a bad feeling about this ... and I think we should go."

Max doesn't argue, and without saying anything more, we turn toward the marina.

There aren't many lights coming from the cottages in the distance anymore, and most of the houseboats are nothing more than dark, ominous shapes on the shore. It isn't really that late, but still, I'm not supposed to take the kayak out after dark.

We paddle side by side, and for a split second, I think I hear something in the water behind me. It's crazy how your ears can play tricks on you when you're freaked out.

When we reach the moored sailboats in the bay, I spot Dock 5 and I think we're home free; that is, until I see my dad and Ben and Nell standing at the edge, waiting. Dad's arms are folded across his chest. This is never a good sign.

"Uh oh," Max says, paddling ahead a little, "I think we're busted. They don't look too happy."

"Ya think?" I scowl. I'm pretty sure they are not going to share my enthusiasm for exploring derelict, abandoned ships in the dark.

"You better have a good explanation, Hannah," my dad says before the three of them turn around and head back up the dock toward our houseboat. Max and I paddle sheepishly alongside in the water.

I glide past our neighbour's houseboat, and snug up beside ours, wondering what I can possibly say to make my father understand. I could just say we got lost out in the dark, which is sort of true.

Nell reaches out and grabs the shock cord rigging on the front of my kayak, holding it steady while I hop out onto the deck. Ben does the same for Max.

"I've been calling your cell for an hour!" Dad's fingers are drumming on his arms. "Aunt Maddie bought you the phone for a reason, Hannah."

I remember that my phone is buried deep in my backpack, zipped inside an old camera bag. "I'm sorry, Dad. I just didn't hear it."

"You lose your marbles, Hannah?" Ben asks. "Why are you out there after dark, anyway?" He switches off his flashlight and just stands there, shaking his head.

Max and I face the three of them and I shift uncomfortably from one foot to the other. I don't get in trouble much, but I just can't let Dad in on all of this. Not with his trip so close.

"You're fourteen now, Han," he says. "This isn't a hint of rebellious days ahead, is it? Because if it is, I'm pretty sure I'm not going to be okay with that."

"No, Dad. Really. We didn't mean to be out there for so long. We were just exploring and got turned around in the dark. Really."

"I'm leaving in two days, Hannah Banana," Dad says. "I hope I'm not going to have to spend my time in Spain worrying about you back here."

Hannah Banana. Man, I wish he would stop calling me

that. It's totally embarrassing and I'm grateful that it's dark, so Max can't see me blushing.

"You do realize that you could have been run over by a boat out there, right?" Ben says gruffly. "You'd have been impossible to see. It happens."

"I know," Max says finally, and then looks at my dad. "I'm sorry, Mr. Anderson. It was my idea to go out. Don't bust Hannah. She was trying to talk me out of it, but I wouldn't listen."

Stunned, I look at Max but he doesn't meet my gaze. Instead, he starts adjusting the strap of his backpack, so that it rides lower on his back. At that moment, the butterflies in my stomach wake up and make their presence known to me in no uncertain terms.

Way to take the bullet, Miller!

Dad just scowls.

"I'm sorry, Dad," I say, meaning it.

"No more shenanigans, okay?"

Shenanigans. Who says *shenanigans*? My father, that's who, and I smile before I think better of it. "Okay, Dad."

"Right. Get on back to the house, then." His tone of voice means the conversation is now closed. It's a voice he doesn't use much, so it sounds strange and unfamiliar.

Later, when I'm lying in bed with Poos and Chuck, one on either side of me, I can't seem to shake a general feeling of rottenness. Even though I apologized to Dad, it's obvious how disappointed he is. I want to kick myself—I should have put myself in his shoes. I vow to make it up to him before he leaves.

But eventually I stop thinking about Dad and start thinking about the *Orca I* again, and no matter how hard I try, I can't ignore the feeling in my gut.

Chapter Twenty

❧

IZZY

EAGLES AND ALPACAS make pretty good companions. At least they seem to like my company. I wish I could say the same thing about my friends back on Salt Spring Island. I've only had one text since I left—from Marika—asking me if she could have some artwork that I left in the school's art room.

And that had been that. There hadn't been any, "*How's it going over there, Izzy?*" or "*We really miss you, Izzy,*" or "*Can't wait to see you, Izzy!*" Nothing. I may as well be spending the summer in Micronesia. Marika can have the stupid paintings. It's just work the rest of the world is sure to mock. Good riddance.

"You have so much potential, Isabelle," my art teacher, Ms. Burns, had said. "These compositions are unique. A real cultural statement, too."

Oh, they're a statement all right. Traditional native designs dragged kicking and screaming into the 21st century, only to be met with a lot of eye-rolling and nose-wrinkling from my mother and some of the elders back home. My art teacher might like my work, but so much for the rest of the world.

Ten minutes later, after I force myself to get up, get dressed, and go up to the cottage for something to eat, I find Ramona is already up. She's standing near the sink, waiting for the kettle to boil. Who did her hair this morning? BC Hydro?

I scrutinize an apple from the wicker basket in the middle of the kitchen table. It's small, with a couple of black spots, so I put it back and select another less organic-looking one. One that doesn't seem as though it might be hiding some sort of disgusting bug I have no interest in meeting.

"Good morning, Iz," Ramona says, yawning. She picks up a stray thread hanging down from the pocket of her baggy, black and white polka-dot shorts and gives it a yank. I can't help wonder if maybe Ramona needs glasses? Her outfits give new meaning to the word "bizarre," and this one is no exception. Along with the shorts, she has on a bright red t-shirt that says "Bellhorn Food Co-op" across the front, and "Organic farming: It's in our Nature" on the back. Of course, she's wearing her customary croc sandals, this pair a nauseating shade of bright orange. On her head, sitting at a slight angle, is a purple crocheted beret. (As if she needed to draw attention to her spastic hair!) But as far as I can tell, Ramona is the norm here. Cowichan Bay is just one big, hemp-fibred, fashion faux pas. I look down at my stovepipe jeans that disappear into my retro Doc Martens. Without question, my Docs are my favourite footwear. I snagged them a year ago at Value Village in Victoria, almost new for fifteen bucks.

"Did you sleep okay?" Ramona asks.

"Sure," I say, even though I didn't. I still haven't fully recovered from my night-time foray into the fog. Not to mention the conversation I overheard between Max and Hannah. What's going on with that old boat, anyway? At least the paddle sitting in a puddle of seawater at the end of the dock goes unnoticed by Ramona.

I change the subject. "Have you seen Two-Step yet?"

"Not yet," she says, "although he was here earlier this morning. The chicks have been quiet for a bit so I guess he must have found breakfast for them."

"Well, I can't stop helping him. Oscar and Tango are going to fledge soon. They'll need to be eating a ton," I tell her.

"Oscar and Tango . . ." Ramona smiles. "Such good names."

She takes the kettle off the stove as it starts to whistle, pausing before selecting the bright pink box of "Utopia Blend" from her drawer full of hippy teas. I suppress a smile as I wonder if a tea that tastes like grass and dirt can actually transport you to paradise.

"This should realign my chi," Ramona says as she places a tea bag into her mug.

Sometimes Ramona can be even flakier than my mom. All you have to do is check out the inside of her house. I look over the window above the kitchen sink, where several glass crystals hang, catching the morning sunlight as they cast rainbow prisms on the lemon-yellow wall across the room. Women like Ramona always have crystals in their windows, and motivational posters in their bathrooms. The one in Ramona's is a night shot of a starry sky that says: *Shoot for the moon. Even if you miss, you'll land among the stars.*

While Ramona waits for her tea to steep, I look out to the ocean. There isn't a puff of wind in the clear, blue sky and the whole bay is peaceful and quiet, so different from last night. That chanting! Those men's voices! And, why did I get so disoriented? What *was* that? And what were Hannah and Max doing out there by that old boat? What do they think is going on there?

Finding my way back to shore had not been so easy, even with my paddling skills. Hannah and Max had been out front, so staying out of sight had been tricky. I am grateful that the *Black Swan* is black.

After finishing her tea, and despite her embarrassing outfit, Ramona walks to the village to run errands. I make myself some toast and take it outside to eat breakfast with Paco and Luna. When I sit down on an overturned pail, the alpacas amble over and push their bony, hairy heads through the fence to investigate my breakfast.

I pull out the half-smoked cigarette from last night and light it up, drawing the smoke deep into my lungs. But when

I exhale, the smoke goes straight into Luna's face and she backs away as though she's been stung by one hundred bees.

"Oh, I'm sorry, Luna!" I jump up and stamp out the cigarette, but both Paco and Luna give me cautious sideways looks and then amble back to their shelter.

"No, really! Come back. I put it out! See?" I tell them, but they ignore me.

Nice going, Izzy. Way to alienate the only real friends you have here!

I pick up the butt and put it inside an empty flowerpot. I should just quit. I can't afford to buy smokes anymore, anyway.

❧

"You again," Riley says when I show up later at the *Tzinquaw*—his fishing boat.

"Me again."

"Sorry kid, no fish today. Try the market?"

"Oh. No. Not yet."

"I hear they have some nice sockeye there."

I nod. Sockeye. Nice maybe, but a little out of my price range. Riley sits himself down in a hammock chair, and is instantly joined by a big grey parrot! I can't help smiling: a salty old sea dog and his trusty parrot.

"I know, I know," Riley laughs, spitting sunflower-seed shells onto the deck. "She belongs to Ben, a friend of mine, but she's a regular visitor—likes her daily fix of sunflower seeds."

"Cool bird," I tell him. "What's her name?"

"Sadie. Sadie? Say hello to . . . to?"

"Izzy."

"Izzy. That short for Isabelle?"

"It is."

Riley leans forward, chewing on some more sunflower seeds. He looks at me with narrowed eyes for at least ten seconds. I never noticed before, but he looks a lot like that country singer. That old guy: Willie Nelson. He's got the same long braid down his back. "Nope," he says finally. "Can't see you as an Isabelle. You look like an 'Izzy' to me."

"I guess I'll see you around," I say as I start to walk back up dock nine, unable to stop the smile spreading across my face.

"Sure thing. Good luck on your salmon quest. Your favourite food or something?"

"Oh," I say, "it's not for me. It's . . . uh . . . I'm helping out some eaglets. Their mom was killed on some power lines." I regret the words as soon as they escape my mouth. Why am I telling this to someone I don't even know? I should know by now that no one really cares what I do. Especially—

"Eaglets?" Riley stands up and Sadie drops off his shoulder to peck at the sunflower husks on the *Tzinquaw*'s deck. "Well, why didn't you say so? I got me a nasty old dogfish yesterday. Tried to throw him back but the poor bugger was too clamped onto my hook. Shame to waste it. Make a fine meal for hungry eagles. You're more than welcome to it."

"I only have a couple of dollars, but—"

"Pffffffft! Keep your money. Dogfish aren't worth anything. Garbage fish. I'm happy to help. I'm heading out for a bit now, but you come back around suppertime. I'll have it in pieces for you."

"That's so nice of you," I say, meaning it.

"Bahhh! No trouble. But I gotta go now. Got fish to fry."

I guess in a manner of speaking, I do, too.

Chapter Twenty-One

❖

HANNAH

"WOW, I SURE HOPE your father doesn't lose his passport," Aunt Maddie says on our way home from dropping Dad off at the airport. She has a point. Organization has never been his strong suit.

"He'll be fine," I say, but I have my own doubts about him as well. When he's deep into a book, his head goes some place else. It can be embarrassing, too, like the time we went through the Tim Horton's drive-thru, and he tried to order our lunch from the garbage can beside the speaker, instead of the speaker!

"At least he has an iPhone now. With GPS, MapQuest, and

stuff. The whole world will be in the palm of his hand." Aunt Maddie laughs, and turns off the main road onto Thain, a gravel road that runs behind Cobble Hill.

"Let's hope he can figure out how to turn it on," I snort. And then add, "Why are we going this way?"

"I know it's a silly detour, but it's just so pretty back here in the early morning. All the second-growth trees."

She's right. Cobble Hill Mountain is wild and beautiful, and the sword ferns that grow along the road behind it are almost as tall as I am. I sink lower in the seat. I'm not really worried about Dad. He'll be okay. I'm going to miss him, but mostly I'm just happy he's getting a real holiday.

"Should we stop up at Valley View for breakfast?" Aunt Maddie asks as we bump along the narrow road. Diluted sunlight filters through the canopy of trees overhead, and a big pileated woodpecker appears on the side of the road, probably searching for ants.

"What's open at 5:30 a.m.?"

"Good point." My aunt stifles a yawn and reaches for her travel mug of coffee. "Why airplanes leave at such ungodly hours in the morning is beyond me."

"I'll get something to eat later when I meet up with Max." Immediately I feel my ears start to burn, although I don't know why.

"Max, eh?" Aunt Maddie says, slyly. "Seeing a lot of him these days, aren't you?"

"He's just a friend. You know, like a brother."

"Oh. Right. *Suurre* he is." She leans over and pokes me in the arm. "This is going to be awesome, Hannah Banana. You. Me. Hanging out together while your dad's gone. There'll be plenty of time for girl talk."

Ugh! Hannah Banana! Puhleeeeze!

"Right. Cool." I squirm in my seat. Why are adults always so nosy?

"Oh relax, kid. I'm just yanking your chain. Just tell it to your diary if you'd rather. I won't bug you."

I bristle at the word "diary." I had managed to forget about mine—at least for a little while. But thinking about Sabrina Webber reading all those words I wrote makes me hot and cold at the same time. By now she's probably showed all her friends. I'll probably be the biggest joke ever when grade nine starts in September.

Welcome to high school, Hannah Banana. How do you like your new reputation? You get to keep it for four whole years!

I snap out of my funk when Aunt Maddie slams on the brakes as a red truck shoots out of nowhere onto the road in front of us! Our jeep skids across the dirt sideways and then comes to rest on the gravel verge. My aunt leans on the horn and cuts the ignition, but the pickup peels away, leaving us shrouded in a cloud of dirt and dust, seemingly oblivious to the fact that he almost nailed us.

"Whoa! That idiot drove straight out of the woods!" Aunt Maddie fans a hand in front of her face and takes a deep breath. "You okay, Hannah?"

"I'm okay," I say with a pounding heart.

But I'm not thinking about how I'm feeling. I'm thinking about that red 4x4, those familiar bumper stickers, and the green garbage bags in the truck bed. That was Kelso's truck. I'm sure of it. What would he be doing driving behind Cobble Hill Mountain at this hour?

❧

"What are you, a private eye or something? Can't we just go chill on the beach or something?" Max asks, looking bored.

"Seriously, Miller. It was that Kelso dude's truck. I'm sure of it."

"You're so paranoid," Max says. "Besides, there's no law that says you can't drive around at five-thirty in the morning."

I sigh. I don't feel like standing around arguing. "Well, I'm going back to that road before I forget where he was. It's just an hour's bike ride. If that."

"There's nothing behind Cobble Hill. Just a couple of farms."

"Still going," I tell him, picking up Mathilda off the ground. "So I guess I'll see you later."

Max sighs and picks up his own bike. "Okay, okay. You win. Let's go."

We leave Cowichan Bay, and within the hour we are crossing over the main road near the dog park to Thain Road, heading in the opposite direction to the way Aunt Maddie drove. It's a long, slow climb up an uneven part of the road, but my legs feel as though they are made of titanium or something. Or maybe it's the Power Bar I ate earlier.

"Just what are you expecting to find out here?" Max asks as we stop for a drink of water next to a hay field at the top of the hill. The sun is hot and the back of my neck is damp and sticky.

"Something," I tell him. "Anything."

"*Okkaaaay*," Max says sarcastically. "That narrows it down."

I aim my water bottle at him and give it a squeeze, soaking the front of his t-shirt.

"Hey!" Max laughs.

"Come on. Let's just get going. We're not that far from where Kelso's truck pulled out."

Max nodds and wipes off his shirt.

"Here. You want to eat this on the way?" I hold out one of Nell's super-sized sausage rolls as a peace offering, but he shakes his head. "Nah, I'm good. Thanks, though."

The road levels out just past the hayfield, and the forest on either side is denser. Tall cedars and fir trees reach up high overhead, and the ground is a thick tangle of bracken fern, Oregon grape, salal and brambles.

"Here!" I say, suddenly stopping when I see the scuffed-up gravel where our jeep slid across the road. "Right here. He drove out between those two trees, from that trail! See?" I point to an overgrown track leading from the road into the bush.

"You couldn't drive a truck down there," Max says.

"It was a 4x4. Those trucks can go anywhere. Look how the ground is flattened here. Coming?"

"Duh!" Max says. "I'm your knight in shining armour."

"My hero," I say with a salute.

"At your service," Max salutes back.

We follow the parallel lines of flattened growth until they come to an abrupt end.

"Now what?" Max asks, as a flicker darts between two trees ahead of us.

"Now," I say, stepping over a rotting log, "we bushwhack."

"Okay. You're the boss. Let's go."

We stash our bikes behind some bushes and walk slowly for ten minutes, stopping every few steps to listen and scan the ground around us before we move on.

But soon, even I have to admit that what we are doing seems a little crazy. "Okay, stop. I have no idea where we're going or why we're going there. I have to think for a minute."

We sit down on a log, and a familiar black shape swoops in between two cedars to land on the limb of a big maple. Jack.

"Well, hey buddy!" I'm glad to see him. As nutty as he's been lately, I always feel as though he's got my back. Especially when I'm in the woods. But today, Jack is in no mood for small talk, and no sooner has he settled in the tree than he takes off again, squawking like a lunatic.

"What's with him?" Max asks, but before I can answer, Jack swoops down, dive-bombs our heads, darts into the air, and then does the same thing again in the other direction.

"What the—"

"Come on!" I stand up and grab hold of Max's t-shirt, pulling him to his feet. "He wants us to follow him!"

We don't have to walk far—under some low-hanging cedar boughs, through a stand of new trees, and past a thick patch of Oregon grape—before we hook up to a narrow deer trail.

And then I see it! Partially concealed by a cluster of wild willows is a young bear. It's on its back, legs splayed out in all directions, a large pool of blood drying in the grass around it. Max and I both gasp in horror. The bear has had its stomach cut open, and the paws have been removed. It is the most horrific thing I have ever seen.

"Max!" I grip his arm hard as the tears well in my eyes. "Who would do something like this?"

"Crap. Poachers," he says, leading me away, his arm round my shoulder.

I pull myself together, and curse myself for not bringing my phone! I need a picture of this. Why am I not thinking things through lately? Something big is going on, and that something is much bigger than the two of us.

"I feel sick." I clutch my stomach, but Max jerks his head to the left and holds his index finger in front of his mouth.

"What?" I hiss.

"I hear something. A motorcycle or something. Listen!"

He's right. Something is in the woods: an engine revs up and then slows down, and there's the sound of twigs snapping and cracking.

"Crap! It's getting closer," I say. "Come on!"

We leave the bear, and duck sideways into the trees, shielding our eyes from the obstacle course of branches and low-lying limbs that threaten to take us down with each step.

"Quick!" Max says. "Over there!" He grabs my hand and yanks me to the right, practically throwing me down in the dirt behind a giant nurse log.

We wait, hardly breathing, while an ATV crashes through a break in the trees and drives by us on the other side of the log. It's headed toward the bear, and I motion to Max that I'm going to take a peek. He shakes his head, but I ignore him and pivot forward onto my knees so I can straighten up.

It's a big green quad with gnarly tires, carrying two men, and one mean-looking Rottweiler, towing a small trailer behind it. I recognize the red hat right away. Kelso! And his partner is the other guy from the hardware store—Buzz—the skinny dude with the tattoo on his arm.

"It's them," I mouth to Max and he creeps up to have a look as well.

When they disappear into the brush, the engine quits.

"Hey, gimme a hand with this mess you made, Kelso! I can't believe you risked doin' it this close to everybody. What if Webber gets wind of this? You're getting sloppy."

"Aw, you let me worry about Ray. Besides, when I heard there was a bear hanging around the bike park, I had to check it out. Webber can mind his own business."

"Dude, it's his business we're messing with!" Buzz argues, then he spits into the bush.

"Hey! I've never dropped the ball. Not once. I know who butters my bread," Kelso snorts. "He even thanked me for all the extra hours I'm working with the harvesting. Says I got a way with plants!"

Buzz laughs. "Hah. Employee of the frikkin' month, eh? Still, sure would be good to get the rest of that eagle family down near the B&B, though."

The *rest* of the eagle family? I get goose bumps all over. The Old Rose Bed and Breakfast is right beside Ramona's. They're talking about Two-Step and Tango and Oscar!

"Hannah?" Max whispers. "Where's the dog? What happened to that dog?"

I quickly glance around. No dog. I look behind us, then to the right—

Max tugs on my sleeve and points to the bush over to the left, and I see the Rottweiler, sniffing the ground, heading our way. He's picked up our scent!

"We have to go. Now," I say.

"We can't. We're trapped."

The dog is now staring in our direction through the bushes. Any moment, he's going to come unglued.

"Han." Max whispers. "What did you do with the rest of that sausage roll?"

Of course! Brilliant! I swiftly unwrap it from the waxed paper.

"Nitro!" Kelso yells from the bush. "Get over here, ya stupid mutt!" When Nitro turns his head toward the sound of his master's voice, I toss the sausage roll overhead as hard as I can. It makes the smallest noise as it passes through the trees before it hits the ground, but the dog instantly goes berserk, crashing through the brush away from us.

"Nitro! Knock it off!" Kelso yells again, and then his ear-splitting whistle cuts the air. "Come on, buddy. We're going!"

The dog lunges at the sausage roll, gulps it down, and races over to the quad.

"What are you eating now, garbage guts?" Kelso kicks the dog, and it jumps onto the ATV. Then they are gone, and all that is left is a cigarette butt, some tire tracks, and a red smudge on the dirt where the bear had been.

Max and I stare at each other. In the silence that settles over the forest, I swear I can actually hear the blood pumping through our veins.

Chapter Twenty-Two

WHEN RAMONA LEAVES to go to a potluck dinner, I go back to the *Tzinquaw* for the dogfish.

Afterwards, I feel like some kind of weirdo walking through Cowichan Bay with pieces of a giant stinky dogfish under my arm, but then I realize that I actually fit right in. No one gives me a second glance. No one, that is, except a blonde girl sitting outside the Salty Dog Café. As I walk past, she stares at me hard, so of course, I stare back.

She's pretty, but in a Barbie-doll sort of way, and she's the first person I've seen around here wearing a decent pair of jeans.

"You're Isabelle, aren't you," she says when I win the staring contest.

"Izzy."

"Oh. Okay. I'm Sabrina."

"Who?"

"Sabreeeeeeena. Webber?" She says this like I should know the name.

"Oh."

"Ramona has been talking about you around town. About how you're some kind of an eagle whisperer or something. What's with the gross fish?"

I could kill Ramona. So much for keeping it quiet. I shift the heavy plastic bag to my other arm. "Bait. I'm going fishing."

"Right, so don't tell me." Sabrina looks over her shoulder at a Lexus parked on the road near the bakery. Whoever is inside honks the horn: three short blasts. "God! My mother is seriously annoying!"

"I can relate," I tell her.

"I have to go. Have fun . . . *fishing.*" She trots toward the car, blonde hair flying out over her shoulders, leaving me standing in her perfume-filled wake. As the car pulls into the road she rolls down the window and yells, "By the way! Killer jeans . . . *Izzy!*"

I don't say anything. The car is gone before I can even open my mouth to speak. Talk about random.

As I'm standing on the corner, a raven flies out of nowhere

and lands on the garbage can in front of me. He's huge, a bit scruffy, and I recognize him immediately. It's Jack, Hannah's bird. He just stares at me, not moving. What's with all the staring in this town? I meet his eyes. No way I will let a bird intimidate me, especially this bird. Didn't his mother teach him any manners? As if reading my mind, he jumps off the trash can and lands in front of me. There's something in his mouth: a feather of some kind.

Jack swaggers closer on pigeon-toed feet like some kind of movie gangster, the feather straight and horizontal in his beak. He drops it beside my left foot and cocks his head, looking at me quizzically as though he is expecting some kind of a conversation.

"Why are you bringing me this?" I reach down to pick up the feather and hold it up for closer inspection. It's brown, and slightly mottled near the base as though it's been splattered with white paint. I know where this feather came from!

Jack is more animated now that I've seen it. He hops madly from foot to foot, lifting his wings slightly, and then he starts to squawk.

I'm no fool. He's trying to tell me something, and yeah, I know my mom's story is just, you know, a story, but still, no matter how hard I try to ignore all this—Hannah and Jack, the chanting out in the fog—it's almost impossible.

"What?" I say as I sit down at one of the picnic tables along the sidewalk. Jack gives me his beady stare, and then hops right onto my knee! He's so close that I can see the intricate crisscross markings on his grey-black legs. I keep very still and don't take my eyes off him. For a brief moment, I wonder if Jack might hurt me—peck my eyes out the way those birds did in that famous Alfred Hitchcock movie. But no, he almost looks like he's trying to talk. I really believe he's trying to communicate with me.

Half of me needs to see where this is going, while the other half thinks I'm becoming as crazy as the people who live in this village. I tip my head to the left, and Jack mirrors me, cocking his to the right.

There is a sudden *screeeeeeeeee*, which startles both of us. Jack drops to the ground, cawing frantically, and sends me running for Ramona's as fast as I can go, the bag of dogfish tight under my arm.

Something is wrong. Something is wrong with Two-Step.

❧

When I reach Ramona's back yard, there is a guy standing at the base of Two-Step's tree. I've seen him before. That leather jacket—

"Hey!" I shout. He turns around as though he's been stung. Yep. It's Buzz—the doofus who tried to sell me pot. "What are you doing here?" I demand.

"Oh, hey there, beautiful. Surprise, surprise. You live here?"

"What's it to you?" I take another step toward him. He's guilty. There's no question about it. I can tell by the way he's fidgeting and unable to stand still.

"Oh, relax. My cat took off today. Thought I heard him up this tree. Little stinker is always runnin' off." He makes a point of craning his head back to look up into the branches of Two-Step's tree. "Nope. Don't see him. Must of been a different tree."

"Well," I say slowly, "maybe you should be on your way, then."

"Or . . ." Buzz says with a sly grin, "instead of rescuing cats, how about I rescue *you*, and you can give me a nice reward, eh?" He swaggers over and stands directly in front of me. He smells faintly of onions, and there's food stuck between two of his yellowed teeth. Gross. My stomach churns.

"How about you get off my property?" I say.

"Your property now, is it?" Buzz says. He sneers at me, and then spits on the ground between our feet. "I didn't know I was on the reserve."

I am speechless. My first impulse is to spit right back at him, but I just stand there, dumbstruck. How dare he speak to me like that? Who does he think he is?

"Get out of here before I call the cops on you," I finally say.

Buzz smirks again and folds his arms over his pigeon-chest. "Yeah? And just what are you gonna tell them? That you want me arrested for looking for my cat?" He laughs like he's just made the biggest joke on the face of the earth, a laugh that quickly becomes a harsh cough.

"I'll tell them you're selling drugs to minors." There. That should do it. Only it doesn't. Buzz reaches into the pocket of his leather jacket for a cigarette, lights one, and blows the smoke in my face. I don't move. I don't even blink. I won't give him the satisfaction.

"Your word against mine, beautiful," he says smugly, "and like they're gonna believe *you*."

"Get out!"

But Buzz doesn't say anything. He just smirks.

I watch as he walks up the driveway. When he gets to the gravel turn-around in front of Ramona's house, that guy in the red 4x4—the one with the lame mustache—appears on the road and stops to pick him up. Does this dude have his own personal driver or something?

I notice a bunch of garbage bags in the bed of the truck.

"Those are bodies," Buzz says as he climbs into the cab of the truck. "You see what happens to people who piss me off?"

"Is that a threat?" My heart starts pounding.

"Lighten up, girl," Buzz says, slamming the door. "You need to find yourself a sense of humour."

The engine revs and they drive away, spraying gravel in all directions, while Paco and Luna bleat loudly from the field at the side of the house.

"I know!" I call over to them. "I don't like him either!"

Chapter Twenty-Three

✤

HANNAH

IN THE DAYS THAT follow our discovery behind Cobble Hill, Max and I lie low. Twice, in the middle of the night, I think I see lights out on the *Orca I*, but I can't be sure. We agree to keep our mouths shut, but keep our eyes open, until we figure out what to do next. I'm glad that work at the Salish Sea Studio has started. It helps to be busy.

Usually I'm pretty good at reading people, but Isabelle Tate is a mystery. Working beside her in the studio everyday, I want to tell her about the guys in the woods. About the bear. That Two-Step, Oscar and Tango might be in danger, but I don't want to tell her about all the other stuff. I don't know if

I can trust her. On the one hand, she's cool. I mean, she would walk through fire for those eaglets and she's a big fan of Paco and Luna, and in my experience people who like animals are usually decent. On the other hand, she's often in a bad mood, and I am really beginning to hate our staring contests. I don't think she likes me much, and I don't think she likes working in the studio with Ramona either. I don't know how anyone could hate it here. All the skeins of brightly coloured wool, the looms, the swatches of woven cloth and all those huge bags of raw fleece stored in big wicker baskets. It's like being in a candy store. Well, it's like that for me, anyway.

We've been working only a week, but so far I'm in charge of carding, or preparing the wool for spinning. I actually like that part. I sit on the black painted bench by the window in Ramona's studio, watching Two-Step fly in and out of the trees while I just kind of go with the flow, cleaning, separating and straightening the wool fibres to get them ready for spinning. My fingers are fast and the electric, tingly feeling I have when I'm around wool never leaves my fingertips. I can almost go on autopilot, letting my hands do the work while my brain daydreams anywhere it wants to go. More often than not I find myself back in Tl'ulpalus, hanging out with Yisella. Remembering random things, like showing her my iPod and my camera while she showed me how to use native plants for medicine, and how to track animals.

Instinctively now I reach up to touch my abalone necklace, the way I always do when I get that electric sensation in my fingertips. I remember how it felt the first few times I picked up the spindle whorl. How energized and focused I became, as if I was under some kind of a spell. I remember how the villagers of Tl'ulpalus said I had the spinning gift. Some of them were scared of me after that, but not Yisella. And even though two years have passed, I miss her. I can't help wondering if she ended up being okay. There were so many changes happening in the village, all those settlers wanting to live on Yisella's family's land. I think back to those dreams I had back then, especially the last one. The one where I saw Yisella reunited with her family and standing on the beach. That's what I cling to—that no matter what happened with the influx of white settlers in Tl'ulpalus, Yisella remained with the people who loved her. Her family. And Isabelle Tate looks so much like Yisella. It just can't be a coincidence. Can it?

Ramona continues her work on a giant woven blanket, all cobalt blues and teals and sea-greens with burnt-umber edging. It's her biggest piece to date, and there is hardly any room for us in the studio because her loom takes up half the floor space. We've been listening to music most of the time, sometimes talking, sometimes not. It's probably the best summer job I could ever have, but it's obvious that Izzy doesn't share my enthusiasm.

Ramona has started Izzy on some traditional Cowichan mittens. They're plain—only one colour change with a simple motif in the centre—and although Izzy can knit, it's evident that she would rather not. Every time Ramona leaves the studio to make tea or answer the phone Izzy throws her work aside and pulls out her sketchbook.

Now, while Ramona has run up to the cottage to bring back some fruit, Izzy opens the book on her lap. There are a lot of strange, intricate line drawings, patterns and textures. I watch over her shoulder as she flips through the pages: twisted trees, fantastical figures and other ones that look like zombies, with missing eyes or limbs. But even though they're pretty weird, they're also pretty good. Technically perfect, I'd say. I lean in a little closer and notice that, along with her drawings are lines and lines of scrawly text, although I can't actually read the words.

"Do you mind?"

I jump. Busted.

"Oh, I wasn't really snooping. I just . . . "

"Yes you were," Izzy says, looking up as Ramona enters, carrying a bowl of cherries. She shuts her sketchbook and drops it into a red canvas bag at her feet. Hanging from the strap are a million tags and decorations, each of which is attached by a lanyard to a silver clip. I notice that one is a tiny bright blue bicycle, which reminds me of Mathilda. It makes me wonder if Izzy likes bikes. Maybe we could go for a bike ride sometime. Maybe that would be easier than trying to talk.

"I didn't mean to be nosy," I tell her, meaning it. "It's just that you're really good."

"Oh. Thanks," she says, a little guarded.

Ramona sets a bowl of cherries down on the other end of

the black bench. "Eat up, you guys. These cherries are to die for!"

Izzy ignores her but I immediately reach over and grab a handful. The cherries are dark, almost black, and incredibly sweet. How could anyone resist these? I eat about a million before I get back to my wool.

We work silently for over an hour. I begin to relax, even daydream, about this afternoon. Max and I are going to hang out in Victoria. Not really a date, but still. I need to fill my head with the noises and distractions of the city so as to replace the image of that bear, which has taken up permanent residence in my head.

When Ramona leaves to pick up her knitting friends who are coming to work with us for the day, Izzy puts down her needles.

"Two-Step," she says out loud but I don't think she's talking to me. "Lunch time." She pushes her fingers through her spiky hair, scratches a bit of black polish off her thumb nail, slides her feet into a pair of red mary janes, and disappears.

Moments later she reappears, carrying a chunk of raw fish, which she places at the base of the big fir tree. When Two-Step appears, he hesitates for a bit before performing his usual hop, hop, hop forward, then two hops back. Although I've seen him do this a couple of times since I started working here, it still cracks me up. Now it only takes a couple of minutes before he starts tearing off chunks of fish to take to the nest above.

Izzy comes back into the studio and rummages through the CDs that Ramona keeps beside the old CD player. She inserts a disc and pauses to adjust the volume. I'm surprised when I hear soft classical piano music. It's not what I expected. I had Izzy pegged as a classic punk rock fan.

She leaves the door of the studio open and turns around to see me looking at her. "What?"

"Oh," I stammer. "Nothing. I just . . . you know, like the music."

"Chopin," she says matter-of-factly. "Nocturne In E Flat Major, Op. 9. No. 2."

I think my jaw drops open. "I didn't know you liked classical stuff."

"I don't mind it," she says. "Chopin rocks. Mozart isn't bad, either. And anyway, the music is good for the eagles."

I nod. She may be right about that.

"How are Tango and Oscar doing?" I ask, picking up my work.

Izzy shrugs. "They're good. Growing fast. I just hope they fledge before too many more people know they're there." She gives me a look, then takes out a cigarette pack and stares at it for a second before putting it back. "Until then, I'll need to keep a close eye on them, that's all."

"I'll keep watching, too," I say. "And Riley is coming this afternoon. He's going to do some work on Ramona's dock, so he can watch them while he works."

"Yeah, Riley's cool," Izzy says, and I see a hint of a smile on her face.

We don't talk much after that, and I retrieve some fleece from the floor and pick it apart, doing my best to separate it into usable pieces, but for once my fingers won't cooperate. When we hear the crunch of car tires on the gravel in front of the cottage, Izzy slouches on her bench and leans heavily against the wall.

We hear laughing, and a moment later Ramona appears, followed by two Cowichan women from the reserve: Rosie and Arlene. Both are regulars at Salish Sea Studio, especially in the long, rainy winter months, when sometimes there can be ten women at a time, all knitting with Ramona. But today it's just Rosie and Arlene, two of the best wool sweater knitters in the valley.

"Hi, Hannah," Arlene says cheerily.

"And this is Isabelle," Ramona indicates with a nod of her head, "my friend Louise's daughter, from Salt Spring. Remember, I told you she was coming to stay for a while?"

The two women nod and smile warmly at Izzy.

"Welcome to Cowichan Bay, Isabelle," Arlene says.

"No one calls me Isabelle." Izzy's face is stony and cold. "It's Izzy."

Rosie and Arlene turn to Ramona, who just shrugs and rolls her eyes. They seem unfazed by Izzy's bad mood, but I notice that after several attempts to engage her in a conversation, they give up and leave her alone.

Later, when we stop for a break, Ramona tells Arlene and Rosie, who are all ears, about Two-Step, Oscar and Tango. I know this will only make Izzy's mood worse, so I'm glad when the conversation shifts from the eaglets, to eagle patterns, to eagle motifs for Cowichan sweaters, to Rosie's friend who is part of the eagle clan up in Haida Gwaii.

Izzy is already tapping her fingers nervously on the window ledge, and when Rosie tries to teach Ramona how to pronounce a difficult Haida word she has just learned, Izzy comes unglued. She jumps up, pushing past everyone in the now-cramped studio, and heads for the entrance.

"Going somewhere?" Ramona asks, and the room fills with silence.

"Anywhere but here," Izzy says, not looking back.

"Something wrong?"

"I'm going for a walk."

How awkward do I feel? I've never been a fan of confrontations. I squirm on my end of the bench, and work at picking imaginary twigs out of the fleece held in my lap. I check my phone discreetly and am relieved to see that it is now officially afternoon. For the first time since starting this job, I'm looking forward to quitting time, and I am determined not to let Izzy spoil this day, or my "date" with Max in town. But I do feel bad for Ramona. Ramona doesn't have a mean bone in her body.

"Well," Ramona says slowly. I can tell she's trying hard to keep calm. "We're not done here, Isabelle."

"It's Izzy! I keep telling you, it's Izzy!"

"All right, *Izzy*."

"I was just wondering," Izzy says coldly, stuffing her hands into the pockets of her tunic, "if you people ever talk about anything, you know, current?"

"Current?" Arlene looks confused, and glances over to Rosie for help.

"Yeah. You know. The here and now?" Izzy looks at me like I'm supposed to agree with her, like we're actually on the same team, but I have no idea what she's talking about. I really don't.

"Like all the good music that's out there, or the best place to get a cup of coffee, or maybe the latest five-star movie?"

"You want to tell us what's bothering you, Izzy?" Ramona asks quietly.

"Yes!" Izzy explodes. "Yes. I'd love to tell you what's bothering me! Why are you all wasting your time trying to learn a ridiculous language that only a handful of people in the entire world speak, anyway? What's the point? All that crap is history! It's dead in the water, Ramona!"

"Crap?" Rosie asks, setting aside the Cowichan toque she is knitting.

"Yes! Crap! You guys are just like my mother and all her friends. Always talking about the past and the 'old ways'. The stupid customs. Those crazy stories. You never—"

"That's enough, Isabelle," Ramona says, holding up both hands like a traffic cop. "You are being incredibly rude. I think you—"

"And *you're* the worst, Ramona," Izzy interrupts. "I don't know why you're so stoked on being half-native. What's the deal with that anyway? You're Scottish, too."

"Izzy," Ramona says, her face reddening. "Rosie and Arlene are Cowichan. I'm half Cowichan. Your mom is Cowichan. *You're* half Cowichan! Don't you care about your roots at all?"

"I'm also half British, Ramona! My dad is from England! You'd be better off if you focused on your white roots instead of your Cowichan ones. You can't bring it back, you know. Just leave it alone."

Nobody says a word while Rosie and Arlene pack up their things and leave, each of them laying a hand on Ramona's shoulder as they pass through the doorway.

"Bye, Hannah," they call to me as they trudge up the stairs, and Arlene gives me a wink to ease my embarrassment.

"Good-bye Izzy," Rosie says, stopping. "I'm sorry you're so angry."

❖

Riley is halfway to the dock with his toolbox and a can of deck stain when Izzy stops him on the boardwalk.

"Riley? Can you watch the eagles for a while, please?"

"Sure thing, Iz," Riley says. "I'll be here fixing that damn dock till dark. Don't you worry about those little bird brains up there."

"Thanks," Izzy calls back as she stomps up to the road. "I owe you one!"

Chapter Twenty-Four

IZZY

HITCHHIKING HERE IS A JOKE. On Salt Spring, it's always a piece of cake. Everyone knows everyone, and it never takes me more than five minutes to catch a ride from Vesuvius down into Ganges.

But things are different in Cowichan Bay. It's mainly tourists coming up from the village, and they look at me, standing on the side of the road with my outstretched arm as though I'm some kind of an axe murderer or something. Am I *that* scary looking?

After twenty minutes, I give up and begin the climb up the big hill out toward Cobble Hill and the highway. There is bound to be steadier traffic a little farther up.

By the time I reach the top of the hill my clothes are sticking to my back and my legs are burning. I stop under the shade of a chestnut tree to catch my breath and reach into my bag for my crumpled pack of smokes, but the cigarette makes me feel worse, and after two puffs I throw it down on the pavement and grind it angrily with my foot.

How am I going to make it through the rest of the summer here? I'll lose my mind! And while I meant what I said back in the studio, I feel bad about the way I said it. Ramona has been pretty cool to me and she didn't deserve that. But Hannah and Jack freak me out more than anything. The way she looks at me! The way she seems so uncomfortable around me. Shouldn't it be the other way around? Shouldn't it be me that's wary of her? I mean, if I were to buy into my mom's "red-haired girl and raven" story she likes so much.

I don't notice the silver Lexus pull over until I hear, "Hey! Izzy! Over here! Want a ride?"

Sabrina Webber is leaning out of the passenger window, holding her mane of blonde hair back with one arm and waving at me with the other.

I walk over to the idling car. It's low and sleek and even from outside the window I can smell leather, along with that new car smell, and that perfume again—a mixture of roses and vanilla.

"Well, hi there," Mrs. Webber says, turning around in the driver's seat. "It's nice to meet you, Isabelle. Reenie said she met you in the village.

"*Mommmmm!* Pu-leez. Don't call her Isabelle. She goes by Izzy."

"Oh?" Mrs. Webber changes the subject. "Well, those are darling mary janes you're wearing, Izzy!"

Darling?

"We're going into Victoria," Sabrina says. She twists a lock of hair quickly around a finger. "Where are you going? You want a ride?"

"You shouldn't be hitchhiking, sweetie," Mrs. Webber says. "You could have been picked up by a crazy person. I'm glad we spotted you. Oh! Will you look at that little Audi sports car parked over there, Reenie? That should absolutely be mine, don't you think?"

I actually laugh out loud when Sabrina rolls her eyes at me and moves her index finger in circles next to her temple, and says, "Come on. Get in."

"What's so funny?" Mrs. Webber says, looking at Sabrina and me from over the top of her giant sunglasses. "I would look great in a car like that."

I don't doubt it. Like the car, Mrs. Webber's skin is shiny and taut, and she is immaculately turned out in perfectly faded jeans, strappy sandals, and a sapphire-blue gauze blouse. A turquoise necklace stands out against the bronze of her spray-tanned throat.

"I'm going into Victoria, too," I say, adding, "just to hang out for a while." Why not? Where else am I going to go?

"That's so cool," says Sabrina. "Let's hang out together!

Mom? You can just drop us off on Government Street and go do your own thing, okay?"

Mrs. Webber raises an eyebrow. "I thought we were going to shop together?"

"*Mommmmm.*"

"Okay," Mrs. Webber says. "All right then. I guess you girls don't want to be seen with an old hag like me."

Again, Sabrina rolls her eyes, but dutifully says, "You're not an old hag, Mom. You look totally amazing."

"Oh stop!" Mrs. Webber laughs. "Although, in the right light, I can sometimes pass for your older sister, can't I, honey?"

"Sure, Mom," Sabrina says, bored. "Whatever. Just drop us on Government Street."

Neither one has even asked me if I have plans of my own.

❦

"So," Sabrina says, watching her mother's car drive away on Belleville Street in front of the Parliament Buildings, "let's go to the causeway." She adjusts the shiny patent leather belt looped through her jeans and looks to me for a response.

"I thought you wanted to go shopping," I say. I am beginning to wish I'd never accepted the ride. My head is pounding from the stream of chatter I had to listen to between Sabrina and her mother for a full hour. They were almost as bad as Mom at carrying on a conversation, talking all the time but rarely listening to anything the other is saying.

"Pffffftttt!" Sabrina snorts. "I just wanted to get out of Cow Bay, you know? Away from my stoner uncle and his creepy friends. I just wanted to get downtown. To civilization!"

Victoria is pretty cool. There is activity and colour in every direction: people sitting on benches, skateboarders, street musicians and buskers, groups of kids, cyclists, tourists with cameras and dog walkers. The streets are moving and alive with a million images and soon there's no room left in my head for my own sorry slide show. It's perfect.

We walk along the crowded streets, weaving in and out of ambling window shoppers until we reach the causeway. Here we buy giant root beer slushies to drink while sitting on the grass of the Parliament Buildings by the inner harbour.

"Why is it so hot, anyway?" Sabrina says, holding the paper cup against the side of her face.

"It's July," I say.

"I know, but this is nuts! It must be thirty million degrees out here."

She does have a point. It's hotter than hot, and there isn't a puff of wind coming off the water. Even the seagulls are quiet.

"Maybe we should head to the mall," Sabrina says. "You know, for the AC alone."

I shrug, knowing that she is not waiting for an answer. I close my eyes, listening to her blab on about grade nine in September, and the cutest boys at school, and how she's getting a new computer before school starts. Man, I wish for anything to make her stop talking. So when a man dressed as a gold prospector approaches carrying several bright yellow tickets in an old metal gold pan, I sit up and take notice.

"Well, well," he says, "it's your lucky day, ladies. I'm giving away free admission tickets to the Royal BC Museum." He points across the grass to the museum. "Only five left."

Sabrina rolls her eyes—she's good at that—but I lean forward and snatch two tickets out of the pan.

"Air conditioning," I say, looking at Sabrina.

"I need to find a bathroom anyway," Sabrina says. "Let's go."

She snatches a ticket out of my hand, picks up her Armani bag and jogs up to the crosswalk before I'm even standing.

"Thanks," I tell the gold prospector, who tips his hat at me. He has a nice face, with the kind of wrinkles happy people get when they're older.

"My pleasure. Enjoy your visit." He heads toward a group of elderly woman drinking iced coffees near the Undersea Gardens.

I stare at the slip of paper: a trip to the museum would be cool, but going with yet another person who has an aversion to silence? I immediately regret snatching the tickets. I mean, I could be sitting alone on a rock near the water, people watching, and enjoying zero conversation. This feels too much like work.

Once we are inside the museum, it's much cooler, and because of our free passes we had been fast-tracked past the snaking line of tourists waiting to purchase tickets.

"I haven't been in here since grade four!" Sabrina squeals.

"We should go to the old town part. That's the coolest. The rest of this place is capital 'B' boring!"

I wouldn't know. I've never been here before. We take the escalator up and then walk down a corridor past a special temporary exhibit of animal taxidermy. Sabrina walks quickly through the display, not even glancing at the silent animals around her, but I am curious about each one I pass. There is a black bear, a Vancouver Island marmot, a raccoon and some other rodent that I've never even heard of. They're all dark and still, and stare at me with glazed acrylic eyes that follow me as I move. I feel as though I am being watched.

Get a grip, Iz! You're losing your mind!

I stop when I get to the last exhibit. It's a bald eagle—its wings outstretched so far that I have to duck to go around. I stare into a yellow eye, wondering how the bird landed here, stuffed full of sawdust and cemented to a piece of granite. It looks so much like Two-Step that I am immediately struck by how stupid it was for me to storm off the way I did. Riley may be cool, but it isn't his job to babysit those birds. I was the one who signed up for the job. Some guardian I turned out to be.

"Come on, Izzy!" Sabrina shouts from the exit door, her voice loud and shrill. I can almost imagine this eagle shuddering at the sound. She waits impatiently, one hand on her hip, phone in the other. She laughs out loud, then skitters across the polished floor to where I am standing, texting all the way.

"Oh my God. Joshua and Brandon are here. Josh just sent me a text!"

"Who?" I ask.

"Josh Talbot and Brandon Kirkpatrick. Hottest guys in the school. They saw us in the lobby." Sabrina digs in her bag, pulls out a mirror and instantly begins to inspect her face for visible flaws. "They totally want to hang out."

I look back at the eagle and its eye bores through me, making me feel guilty. They're all staring at me: the marmot, the raccoon, the bear . . . judging me . . . watching me . . .

Pull yourself together, Izzy. They're stuffed animals!

"Hullo? Earth to Izzy? Would you quit looking at those dead animals and pay attention?"

When I don't, she just sighs and says, "Okay. Whatever. I'm just going to go down to the lobby and meet them, okay? I'll come back in ten minutes. Wait here." She is halfway to the escalator before I even agree. Then she's gone, and it's only me, and a room full of animal ghosts that are totally creeping me out. I hitch my bag up on my shoulder and walk quickly past them, through the archway and into the history section.

I round the corner and walk through a narrow passageway to find myself in the "First Peoples of Canada" exhibit, looking at the timber structure of a large pit house—a replica of one that was discovered near Anahim Lake in the interior. From hidden speakers somewhere comes a low, steady drum beat accompanied by faint chanting. It sounds exactly like the chants I heard out on the water, but I can't tell where exactly the sound is coming from.

All around me are glass cases filled with artifacts and archival photos. Where *is* everybody? There was such a big line-up in the lobby; I can't be the only one interested in this floor but I don't hear anything except the drums.

Something catches my eye in the centre of a nearby case. I move closer until I am only inches away from the glass. Inside is a strange circular disc. It is wooden, burnished and smooth, about the size of a dinner plate, with a small hole, not much bigger than a nickel, in its centre. I feel the urge to reach out and touch the wood, to trace my fingers across the two arched salmon carved head-to-tail around the hole in the centre. The bottom of the disc is slightly damaged, and some of the carved imagery has been worn away.

When I read the placard placed beside it, a thrill runs down my spine.

SPINDLE WHORL
Recovered from Tl'ulpalus, Coast Salish (Cowichan)
culture, Cowichan Bay, BC (19th c.), maple wood

"It's beautiful, isn't it?"

I jump and turn to see a woman standing behind me. She is smiling, beaming in fact, and her eyes are dark and shining. She must work on this floor. A kind of tour guide, or interpreter or something because she's dressed in traditional First Nations clothes: a cedar cone-shaped hat, a woven bark poncho, skin boots, and a cedar skirt. Her hair falls down her back in a thick black braid.

"Sure," I say, finding my voice.

"Sort of has a way of mesmerizing you, doesn't it?" the woman says.

"Kind of."

"Are you from the Island? The Cowichan Valley, perhaps?"

I take a step backward and search for the glowing red exit sign. How would she know where my family's from? "Um. Do you work here?"

The woman doesn't answer. She just keeps smiling fondly at me, like she's an old friend or a kindly aunt or something. Either that or she's not quite right in the head. Probably the latter. The world is full of crazies.

"What do you think of the exhibit?" she asks, finally moving away toward a case full of black and white photographs, some grainier than others.

"It's okay, I guess. It's kind of dark in here, though. And what's with the noise? Did they just turn up the drum beats or something?" The atmospheric music is loud. Whoever the museum's tech support person is, they are clearly falling down on the job. It's almost as though the drummers and chanters are right in the room with us; it feels too much like my night paddle in the kayak.

The woman doesn't answer. She's too busy studying the photographs.

"That's where I'm from," she says when I'm right behind her. "That's my family's village. Tl'ulpalus."

"Tu . . . what?"

"Tl'ulpalus. Some people call it Kilpalus. There are a few different ways to say it, and spell it, too." She points to a photo of several men standing next to their large canoes on a beach. The photo was taken in front of six or seven longhouses. "That was the village where the town of Cowichan Bay is now. There's a marina there, and lots of shops. I still visit from time to time. It's not far from here, maybe an hour. Do you know it?"

I feel like my mouth has been glued shut. I lean in to study the photograph more intently, trying to see past the grainy sepia tone of the photograph to the blurry details in the background. It looks to be mostly tall trees, but there are several welcoming poles in front of the longhouses, facing out toward the sea.

"It was my family's home for generations," the woman says. "And that spindle whorl? It came from my village. There were stories told about it that my grandmother told to me. It is very special." The woman lowers her voice, as though she is about to reveal a secret of huge significance. I look at the whorl, not quite sure what I'm supposed to see, or feel, but nonetheless, my eyes lock on to the images of the salmon, their curved bodies chasing around the hole in the centre. As I stare, the salmon begin to move, slowly at first, and then so fast that the carving begins to blur and spin. I rest a hand against the side of the cabinet to steady myself, but I can't look away. Around and around the whorl spins, faster and faster, until I feel my stomach lurch and shift and my legs grow weak. For a second I think I might throw up.

At that moment, I feel hand on my shoulder. The whorl and my stomach stop spinning, and my head begins to clear.

"It moved for you, didn't it?" the woman asks.

"What? No! I don't know what you're talking about."

"Hah!" the woman laughs, "so stubborn. Just the way I was when I was your age. Until I stopped to listen, that is."

I blink at her. What's with the cryptic talk? Who does she think she is? She doesn't know anything about me! I feel suddenly confused and angry. "I have to go," I say. "I'm meeting someone."

"Your friend?" The woman removes her hand from my shoulder and smiles. "Ah yes, she's downstairs. I had better go now, too." She turns and walks toward the exit on the other side of the room. Just like that.

"Wait!" I yell and she stops, but doesn't turn around.

"Yes, Isabelle?"

"What's your name?"

The woman hesitates for a moment before saying, "Taatka. My name is Taatka."

And then she is gone. I hurry back, down the narrow passageway toward the escalators. Then I stop in my tracks. How did she know my name?

Chapter Twenty-Five

❦

HANNAH

I DON'T CARE HOW long we have to wait in line for tickets at the museum because I'm having a day off with Max.

I sneak a look at him standing beside me. He's kind of dressed up, wearing a new white t-shirt, black and white board shorts, and a pair of stiff-looking (new) sandals. I think there might be stuff in his hair, too, although I can't be sure. It could just be sweat. It is blistering hot out today.

Aunt Maddie said my wrap skirt and Indian cotton camisole looked "feminine without being foo-foo," and I'm pretty sure that's a good thing.

It takes us fifteen minutes to inch our way up to the counter, to where a stern-looking older woman watches us across the top of her bifocals.

"Two youth? Eighteen dollars, please."

I reach for my wallet, but Max places a hand on my wrist and says, "Nope. I'm getting this."

"It's okay," I tell him. "I have money. You don't have to—"

"Hannah?" he smiles. "I want to. Quit being a control freak, okay? You can pay next time we go out."

Next time we go out. I feel myself flush, as I stuff my wallet back in my purse. I'm used to carrying a backpack, so carrying Aunt Maddie's Mexican embroidered bag feels strangely alien. Not bad really, just different.

"There are people waiting behind you, kids," the woman says, but she isn't really mad. She looks like she's trying hard not to smile.

Max gives her a twenty-dollar bill and waits for the toonie change.

"Thanks," I tell him, as we move through the main doors to the escalator.

As we ride up, Max takes my hand and gives it a squeeze. My stomach, true to form, performs an impressive backwards somersault.

"Remember when we came here to meet Mr. Sullivan? After you found the spindle whorl? I'd only known you a week or two back then."

How could I forget? We went with my dad, and spent the day in Victoria.

"Let's go to the simulated forest," Max says, straightening

up. "Come on. It'll be just like old times. A little nostalgia."

So that's what we do and I can't help thinking how nice this is. Sort of romantic, even though we were only twelve then and more interested in the stuffed cougar than holding each other's hands.

When we get to the forest, it's exactly the way it always is. Twilight-ish, and cool, with background sounds of birds and the wind rustling in the trees. We make a beeline for the cougar, and then for the big grizzly bear ripping away at the decomposing log, his long, formidable claws raking away at the bark. And while this bear makes me think about the mutilated bear, being farther away from that secret in the woods, the unsavoury characters and derelict boats feels good. I needed a day like this.

Max squeezes my hand again and we walk out of the forest, toward the Museum's "old town." We are almost at the escalator when we see Sabrina Webber talking to Josh and Brandon, two boys from school. She is laughing too loud (big surprise) and playing with her hair, and both Josh and Brandon look like goofy dogs waiting for a canine cookie.

She does a double take when she sees Max and me, and I half expect Max to let go of my hand but instead he grips it tighter.

Sabrina drops her eyes to our hands, and then gives Max one of her killer smiles. "No. way! No. WAY! You guys are going out? Oh, that's so cute!" She runs over to us and tries to envelop us in some kind of bizarre group-hug thing, like we've been best friends since kindergarten. Ew.

"So, you guys. Izzy is here with me. She's upstairs some-where, but she's like, totally being weird. She's zoned out in front of the dead animals up there. Probably stoned or some-thing."

"Izzy came here?" I say. "She's in town?"

"Hullo? That's what I just said. She came in with me. We gave her a ride. Are you even listening to me, love-struck Hannah Banana?" Josh and Brandon snicker, and I feel my cheeks burn.

That proves it! The only way Sabrina could know about *Hannah Banana* is if she did take my diary, so I call her on it.

"And just how do you know about that nickname?"

She remains composed, but I think I see her twitch ever so slightly.

"Oh. Who knows? I just do."

"Only three people call me that."

"Really?"

"Yes. Really."

She doesn't say anything more and neither do I, but I keep staring straight at her blue eye-shadowed eyes. She knows I know. Hah! Score.

Max drapes his arm around my shoulder and I lean against his side as I feel myself melt. Is it that easy? Can a simple half-hug diffuse Sabrina-infused tension this fast? I give him an appreciative smile, which he happily returns, but then I look back at Sabrina and replace mine with a stony stare. She breaks first, and her gaze drops to her pink painted toes. Hah! I win again!

Karma, Miss Webber. You'll get yours.

When Izzy strides purposefully across the floor toward us, I stop thinking about Sabrina and my diary because again I am struck by the likeness. She is just so like Yisella! The way she walks with her back poker-straight and her chin stuck out in front of her. The way she looks as though she knows exactly where she's going and why. "I thought you were coming back?" she says to Sabrina.

"Oh, yeah, but . . . " Sabrina gestures to Josh and Brandon as if to illustrate that they are a perfectly acceptable reason to forget about the time.

"Well, I'm done with this place," Izzy says.

"Aww. Those frozen critters get to you?" Sabrina says, smirking. "You should have seen her, guys. She was completely messed up. It was hilarious."

"I ended up in the First Nations section," Izzy says, "but I was followed around by this whack tour guide who wouldn't shut up about all the artifacts."

"Really?" Brandon says, his eyes growing wide. "That exhibit is open?" He exchanges a look of disbelief with Josh, and then adds, "That dude over there told us that section is closed for renos or something. See? There's the sign."

FIRST PEOPLES OF CANADA EXHIBIT

CLOSED FOR RENOVATIONS.
OUR APOLOGIES FOR THE INCONVENIENCE.
PLEASE VISIT AGAIN.

"Well," Izzy says frowning. "Obviously that's an old sign, because I was just there!"

"Cool!" Brandon says, splitting away from us. "I want to see it. There's wicked stone tools and stuff in there. What do they call it? Lithic technology or something. Anyway, it's awesome. Let's go, Josh."

Sabrina skitters after them, her heeled sandals tapping a staccato beat across the tiled floor. "Wait, we'll go back up with you guys."

"We will?" Izzy raises an eyebrow, and I wonder if she's thinking what I'm thinking: so much for playing hard to get.

"Izzy? Just come on!"

"May as well," Max whispers to me. "We can see the spindle whorl again."

I'm definitely up for that. It's been over a year since I've seen it, and it never gets old. Each time I look at it, it's like I'm seeing it again for the first time, and I feel that crazy adrenaline rush I felt the first time I touched it. And while its discovery led me to Yisella and all the hardships she had to face, at least I can take comfort in knowing that her mother's prized spindle whorl is safe from danger. If it couldn't remain safely with her family, at least it can be preserved here.

We follow the others up the escalator, and then through the dark room of taxidermy. It is a little unsettling, all those still and silent animals, perched just so, watching us walk by. I can see why Izzy might have been a little wigged out.

There are sawhorses obstructing the exit, and yellow tape blocking off the entire section in all directions. Sabrina holds her thumb and forefinger to her lips, as though she is smoking, and says, "Um, Izzy? Girlfriend? A few too many tokes, maybe?"

Izzy stares at the sawhorses in dismay. "This isn't possible. These were NOT here five minutes ago. I walked right through here. I walked right through and over to that exhibit. There was this museum interpreter dressed in First Nations clothing. She talked about her old village. She—"

"*Riiiiiight,*" Brandon says. "Sure you did."

"No!" Izzy barks. "I'm telling you! This wasn't here!"

"Come on, Izzy," Sabrina says. "It doesn't matter. Let's just go. We can go down to Beacon Hill Park or something. Maybe go down to the beach and lie in the sun—"

"NO!" Izzy pushes past us and in between the sawhorses.

"You're gonna get busted!" Max calls after her.

"Wouldn't be the first time," she says coldly, not stopping.

I look at the others, just standing there like dopes, and follow after her. I know what it's like to have people think you're half-crazy. Think you're making up stories. I know that better than anyone!

I push past the sawhorses, even though Max makes a grab for my hand and misses.

"I'll be right back," I say sharply. I can't help remembering that Max still isn't one-hundred percent convinced about my own story.

I follow Izzy around a corner and down a narrow passageway and then we come to the exhibit's entrance. There is no lighting other than the few emergency lights glowing overhead. All the glass cabinets are covered with white drop sheets, and there are paint cloths on the floor against one of the far walls. Several ladders lean up against a wall, and paint trays are scattered here and there in the centre of the room. The place is definitely closed.

Izzy looks around in all directions over and over, as if expecting to see something or someone materialize. She turns to me. "This is nuts, Hannah. I was just here. I was standing right over there!" She points at a particular case.

"That one?" I know that display case. I know that case better than any of the others. It's the one with the—

"I was looking at a spindle whorl. It's from Cowichan Bay, found near the village or something. I remember it perfectly. It's maple, with salmon carved on it, and the woman said she was actually from there. She said her ancestors lived there in a village called Tl'ul . . . Tl'ulp . . . "

"Tl'ulpalus?" I say, my voice trembling slightly.

"Yes! Tl'ulpalus. It was near where the marina is today. I swear to God, Hannah. I am NOT making this up."

We see the others coming down the narrow passageway, and Izzy clamps her mouth shut. "Don't say anything!" she hisses at me. "Promise!"

Before anyone says a word, a man dressed in coveralls and a painter's cap appears from another corner, looking less than pleased. "Hey! You kids can't be in here. This exhibit is closed."

"Oh. Right. Sorry," Max says, "my friend sort of got lost."

"Well, take your friend and out you go! This won't be open

for another couple of weeks. You're lucky it was me who caught you in here."

We all turn to go back downstairs, all except Izzy, that is. She hesitates for a moment and then approaches the man with the paint roller. "Excuse me," she says, "but can you tell me where the woman who works here went?"

"Woman?" the man says. "Josie's usually the only one, but she's on holiday right now."

"No," Izzy says, frowning. "I mean the woman dressed in First Nations clothing? The interpreter who works here? She said her name was Taatka."

"Who? You're seeing things, kid. We don't have costumed interpreters here, not like the bigger museums in, say, Ottawa. Not enough money in the budget."

"So you don't know Taatka?"

"Nope. No one up here except me and Conroy, and Conroy hates teenagers, so I'm pretty sure you didn't share a conversation with him. Now please, everyone, it's time to leave. I've got to get back to work."

Everyone looks at Izzy as if she's lost her mind, before they turn and walk away. Everyone except me. I look at her face, and she looks at mine, and I know that look—the one of amazement, disbelief, fear and uncertainty.

"Izzy?"

She stares at me with wide eyes, but says nothing.

"I believe you," I tell her. And I do.

Chapter Twenty-Six

✦

IZZY

"NEXT TIME YOU DECIDE to take off for no reason, you think that maybe you could let me know?" Ramona asks when I come through the door well past dinnertime. She has her back to me at the kitchen counter, and is angrily grating carrots into a bowl of cake batter in front of her.

"I didn't plan it. I just went. I just got frustrated. I . . . I needed to get away for a while." I'm sitting at the kitchen table, tearing up a paper napkin into a mountain of tiny paper curls.

"You were really rude to Arlene and Rosie."

"I know," I say, because it's true. I was. "I'm sorry, Ramona."

"Well, if you're going to work here this summer, Isabe—

Izzy, you'd better work on your attitude."

"This was my mother's idea. Remember? Not mine."

Ramona puts down the knife and turns to look at me. "Well, you don't have a choice on this one." I've never seen her so serious. "You could try to make the best of it, you know," she says.

"You don't understand. Amelia needs me. Mom is always so busy being a big fish in a small pond. It totally sucks. You wouldn't know unless you were around our house. It's not like Mom means to ignore us. She just likes helping other people so much that she sometimes forgets about us. It doesn't matter with me so much, but Amelia is only seven."

Ramona is quiet as she continues to grate carrots. For a while, she just chops and I shred napkins, because there doesn't seem to be anything more to say. It is what it is.

"Do you know someone called Taatka?" I ask out of the blue.

"Taatka?" Ramona turns around to face me, and her eyes grow wide.

"Yeah," I say.

"Why do you ask?" She scoops up the carrot tops and puts them in the open compost bucket on the counter.

"Just someone I met in town. She said her family used to live here a long time ago." It sounds believable, I tell myself. No way I'm going to tell Ramona about the museum. She'd start dancing around and burning sage and howling at the moon or something for sure.

She rinses the knife, places it in the dish rack, and then turns to look at me. "Iz? Do you *know* about Taatka?"

"What do you mean?"

"Your mom never told you stories about her?"

"Well, if she did," I say, "I don't remember. I don't always listen, especially to all the names. They're hard to pronounce."

"Well, you should ask her about Taatka," she says, smiling just a little.

"Why?"

"Taatka was special. Taatka, Miss Izzy Tate, was your mom's great-grandmother, from the village of Tl'ulpalus. Just down the way a bit."

"Stop messing with me, Ramona." Is everyone in Cowichan Bay possessed or something? Is there something in the water that makes people psycho?

"I'm serious. Taatka was a great artist. And a bit of a bad ass in her younger days, I hear."

"How so?" I push the pile of shredded napkins away and fold my arms across my chest. I may as well listen. The eagles are resting so I'm off duty for the moment.

"She was sorta like you, as far as I can tell," Ramona says. "She didn't much care for rules or traditions. Kind of did her own thing, and made a lot of the elders mad when she was a kid. Lots of rule breaking. She was stubborn as a mule."

"How do you know this stuff?"

"You're not the only one your mom tells family stories to, you know. The difference is, I actually listen to them."

"Well she's obviously not the same person," I sigh. "Two people with the same name, that's all."

"Perhaps," Ramona says. "Or maybe Taatka was just checking in to see how you're doing."

I grunt.

"Things generally happen for a reason, but I wouldn't over-think it too much. It's better sometimes just to take the good stuff and say thank you."

"I don't get it."

"Well," Ramona says, "what good came of that little visit? What did you get out of it?"

Okay. I'll play. If I don't, I'll never hear the end of it. I think long and hard, trying to remember every single word that Taatka and I said to each other, standing in front of that display case of artifacts.

"She just said I was stubborn. She said she was stubborn at my age, too. Until . . . "

"Until?"

"Until . . . what did she say? Until she stopped to listen, or something like that. She was kind of rambling. I think she was kind of senile. Probably Alzheimer's. She *was* pretty old."

Ramona wipes her hands on the front of her apron, looking a little smug. "Hmmmm . . . ," she says, "until she stopped to listen, eh? Smart woman." She turns around, leans back against the counter and sticks her hands into the pockets of her skirt. Here we go. I brace myself. I'm pretty good at reading body language, and I understand Ramona's because she's adopted a stance my mother often takes. Usually, when I'm about to get an earful. But Ramona doesn't say a word, which is amazing considering. Instead she just smiles and then turns back to chopping vegetables.

I go out to the deck and replay my conversation with Taatka again, going over everything I can remember, until a knock on the door breaks my concentration.

It's Hannah, standing on the mat with her hands tucked in the back pockets of her jeans.

"Hey, Han," Ramona says. "What's up?"

Hannah grins. "Um. I was just wondering if Izzy is around?"

"Sure. Come on in."

I watch as Hannah follows her into the living room, carefully stepping over a basket filled with some kind of orange flower heads. Ramona always seems to have some kind of plant drying or hanging in her house somewhere. This morning I had to move some straggly looking plant that was suspended over the bathroom sink in order to brush my teeth. I have no idea what it was, but it smelled like cat pee. Charming.

"You want to go down to the bakery for end bits before it closes?" Hannah asks me when I come in from the deck.

"For what?"

"End bits. They're the leftover bits of baking that Nell can't sell. You know, like when she makes a big pan of Nanaimo bars. There's always a strip left around the edge of the baking pan. Perfectly delicious, but not okay to sell. It's the same with all her squares. She saves them for me and for the other kids, too. And today was Nanaimo bar day."

I look at her curiously. She's nervous, that's why she's talking so fast, but I get that. We both know we need to have a conversation. About what happened at the museum. About . . . stuff.

"Sure," I say. "I'll get my shoes. Ramona? Would you mind keeping an eye on the eagles for a little while?"

"I'm on it!" Ramona says.

"Thanks."

Hannah and I walk into the village in silence, both of us unsure how to start the conversation. When we reach the Toad in the Hole, Nell gives us a too-big bag of end bits. Jack waits for us, perched on the edge of the big hanging basket suspended above the door. He flaps off and lands close to our feet, matching our step with his distinctive, pigeon-toed walk. A couple of people pass by and point at him, chuckling. Hannah doesn't seem to notice. I guess she must be used to it.

But raven or no raven, true legend or not, the more I ignore whatever this is, the weirder it's going to get. So I just say it. I just blurt it out.

"You're her, aren't you?" It is more of a statement, than a question.

"Who?"

"You're that girl. You're the girl in the story my mother likes to tell. The one her grandmother used to tell her."

Hannah's face gets redder. "I don't quite know what you're talking about." She stops and sits on the stone retaining wall, finding a space between a mass of pink and orange trailing flowers.

I know she's lying, so I sit down beside her and take a deep breath. Okay. Here goes. "My mother likes to tell this story at family dinners and stuff. It's not exactly a legend, because our family is the only family that tells it, and lots of the other people in the band think my mother is a bit of a nut bar, and if you really want to know, she kind of is."

Hannah waits, watching Jack fly up to the bakery's roof and then head out over the ocean. He never seems to stay in one place for long.

"Anyway," I go on, "the story takes place just over 150 years ago, when white people were starting to settle on Vancouver Island. Apparently, in my mother's village of Tl'ulpalus, this red-haired girl showed up dressed in strange clothes, and she had a raven with her. Some girl from the future. I know! Don't look at me like that. It's whack, right?"

Hannah stays quiet, but picks off one of the orange blooms and dissects it on her lap.

"So anyway," I continue, "this girl supposedly makes friends with one of the girls in the village—my great, great . . . I don't know, great grandmother times six or something. And, well, they can understand each other because of this raven and they end up running away together from some ship full of European dudes. The *Hecate*, I think it was called. Something like that. The story changes every time my mother tells it, but I think I mostly got it right." I look at Hannah, waiting for some kind of response.

"I . . . I . . . " Hannah stammers.

"What?"

The air between us feels charged. Prickly. I rub the top of my head, spiking up my hair. It's something I always do when I'm anxious.

"There's something else," Hannah says slowly, staring out to sea.

"What?"

"Yeah. Do you remember when we first saw each other? By the tree, when you were bringing that fish for Two-Step?"

"Hard to forget. You were like, petrified of me or something. I mean, I'm not *that* weird looking."

"No. It's not that, I just . . . I couldn't stop staring. It's just that you look so much like her."

"Like who?" This feels like twenty questions.

"Yisella. That was her name. The girl in Tl'ulpalus. Because I *am* that red-headed girl, Izzy. It *was* me. I don't know why it happened, and sure don't understand how, but it *was* me. And I met this girl named Yisella. And you look exactly like her."

As she tells me this, the tension between us disappears.

And then she tells me *everything*.

Chapter Twenty-Seven

❧

HANNAH

WHEN IZZY AND I FINALLY stop talking, it's dark. How can two hours pass by so quickly? How can you not notice things like stores closing up or the sun setting behind you?

The relief is huge. Now we don't have to stare at each other like circus freaks anymore. Izzy knows I was in Tl'ulpalus, and I know she's part of Yisella's family, and once I recover from the shock, I actually feel sort of good. This is huge. This means that Yisella had a family. And her family had their own families. It means Yisella stayed safe. For two years I'd hoped that she had managed to survive the invasion of the white settlers, and I had clung to my abalone necklace as a sign that she had.

Yisella had said she would take it off only when she felt safe, that she'd pass it on when she no longer felt she needed protection. So someone else could benefit. And Jack had brought it straight to me on the day I returned to my own life. Now I know its true for sure. Yisella was okay! The worry I've always felt over her welfare finally melts away.

Izzy reaches for my necklace and turns the iridescent piece of abalone over in her hand. "It's really beautiful. Have you honestly never taken it off?"

"Not in two years," I tell her.

She studies it for a while, and there is a softness about her face that wasn't there before. Now she looks more like Yisella than ever.

"I guess I'd better get back," she says.

"Yeah," I tell her, "me, too. But, it's good to tell you that stuff, Izzy. Like, Max, well, he's my friend and everything, but I'm not so sure he totally believes me about what happened."

"You told him?"

"He was waiting for me outside the cave when I, you know, came back."

"Who else did you tell?"

"No one. You're the only other person."

She nods.

When I start walking toward Dock 5, she says, "Hannah? Can I tell you one more thing?"

"Of course."

"There's this dude in town. He tried to sell me pot when I

first got here. I think he might be bad news."

"What do you mean?"

"I think he's up to something. I think . . ."

I halt by the gate. "Is there a red truck involved? Was he wearing a red hat?"

She nods. "Not exactly, but the guy who picked him up drove a red truck, and yeah, he had on a red baseball cap. Anyway, this dude's name is Buzz."

Buzz? Of Buzz and Kelso? "I know those guys!" I tell her. "Well, I know there's something off about them. And I also think Sabrina's uncle, Ray Webber, might be mixed up with them."

"You mean the guy who's supposedly salvaging the *Orca I*?"

"Yeah. I don't think he's the hero everyone's making him out to be. Listen, it's getting dark. Can you come down to our houseboat so we can talk some more?" I need to tell her about those guys, and about what Max and I found behind Cobble Hill Mountain. And it's okay now, because I know she's on our side.

Chapter Twenty-Eight

IZZY

HANNAH'S AUNT HAS gone to a movie with a friend, so we have the houseboat to ourselves. It's not fancy, and nothing matches, but that's the good thing about it. It feels like the kind of place where you're allowed to put your feet on the coffee table or eat dinner on your lap.

Hannah tells me about Buzz and Kelso, the red truck and the presents from Jack. My head feels about to burst when she finally stops talking.

"Does Ramona know about Buzz?" she asks me, handing me some tea in a blue ceramic mug.

"No way. And we can't tell her about these suspicions. It

would only stress her out big time. She can be sort of high strung." I sip the tea. It's good: cinnamon and apple. "Buzz is full of crap. He was interested in the eagles, not me."

"And I'm pretty sure there's more going on out there than just salvaging the *Orca I*," says Hannah. "I *know* I saw two guys out there that morning, in a big orange zodiac. And Jack. Jack hangs out there all the time." She twists her hair nervously over her shoulder.

She looks a lot like the woman in the photograph on the bookshelf across the room: a slender woman with the same red hair. It must be Hannah's mother.

As though on cue, Jack appears on the scene, flying in silently on black wings to "tap tap tap" on the glass with his beak.

"Jack!" Hannah hisses. "Cut it out!"

But Jack keeps doing it until Hannah and I get up and go outside. That's when he drops something with a clatter at our feet. Hannah picks the object up and holds it under the light, turning it over in her hand.

"Check this out, Izzy," she says to me, and I lean over to see. It's a piece of shell. Of abalone, similar in colour to the piece Hannah wears around her neck. It's pretty mucky and still smells a bit fishy, but the swirls of sea-green, turquoise and deep indigo peek through the sand and caked-on dirt, winking under the light.

"Hoo boy . . . so this is present number six," Hannah says, looking at Jack, who is perched on the deck chair. "First I get a cigar butt, then a beer cap, then an eagle talon, an eagle feather, a bear claw, and now this! Duh! It's so obvious!"

"It is?"

"Yeah! Think about it. Eagles? Bears? Now abalone? The fact that Jack is obsessed with the *Orca I*?"

I wait for her to go on.

"Have you read the newspapers lately?"

"Poaching?" I say, remembering the article I read the day I arrived at Ramona's.

"Yes! Elk up Mt. Prevost," Hannah says. "Bear claws . . . Oh, Izzy, you should have seen that poor thing! And isn't the abalone on the west coast endangered?"

"And you think Sabrina's uncle is part of that?" I ask.

"I don't know. Most people in town think he's some kind of God, but if he's hanging out with Buzz and Kelso, I seriously doubt that's the case." Hannah frowns. "I think I need to go aboard the *Orca I*."

"Well, count me in," I tell her, realizing that I may have misjudged Hannah Anderson. She isn't scared, or weird at all. "When?"

"Well," Hannah says, "we have to keep this on the down low. We have to go when no one is awake, like in the middle of the night. Max and I paddled out there once before."

"I know, I was out there, too. On the same night. Only I hid when I saw you two coming. You're not the only ones who like to kayak at night." I don't tell her about the chanting or drums though.

"You were?" Hannah's eyes grow wide. "I *knew* I heard a splash near the boat."

"Yeah," I say. "Probably me."

"Okay, so listen. We need to make a plan. To go back. Only this time we have to get on the ship. And we can't tell anyone about this. Deal?"

"Deal," I say, adding, "what about your boyfriend?"

"Not even Max. If we—"

"What do you mean, '*not even Max*?'" Our conversation is interrupted by a voice that is definitely not female. Max jumps onto the houseboat deck dressed in a pair of oversized jeans and a dark hoodie. He holds out a paper bag. "Donuts. No need to thank me, ladies, even though I just spent my last six bucks." He hands us the bag and settles himself into a chair. "I was looking in the village for you, Han. You aren't answering your cell again." He reaches into the bag and pulls out a chocolate-frosted long john.

Hannah shifts on her feet. "Oh! Max! I, uh ... I forgot to check. Izzy and I were just hanging out."

But Max is hardly listening. Instead he's breaking off crumbs from his donut and tossing them to Jack who is clearly impressed. "So what do you mean, 'not even, Max?'"

"Huh?" Hannah says, raising her eyebrows at me when Max isn't looking.

"Come on, Anderson. You guys were talking about me. I'm not an idiot."

Hannah and I exchange looks. I don't say anything because this is Hannah's deal. And, seeing as I've never had a boyfriend, I'm not sure how it works.

"Oh, *all riiiiight*! I guess you may as well be in on this. Come on inside."

We follow Hannah back into the living room, leaving Jack to enjoy the rest of the long john.

⚜

"A camp-out, huh?" Ramona says the next morning, taking a clothes peg out of her mouth. It's a crystal clear day. Windless, cloudless—perfect for kayaking.

I hand her a couple of damp pillowcases from the hamper on the deck, and she pegs them expertly to the clothesline.

"Hannah said there are tons of nooks and crannies over there in the shadow of Mt. Tzouhalem, near Skinner Bluff, and it's the easiest paddle ever. We thought we could pitch a tent and then paddle back in the morning. Come on, Ramona. It's a perfect day, and we're both great kayakers."

Ramona doesn't answer right away. Instead she puts her arms out, waiting for more laundry. I pass her a bundle of sheets, all of them white and covered with tiny blue flowers. She hangs them side-by-side, until all I can see are her croc-covered feet between the spaces, and the red and white bandana that is tied around her forehead.

"Come on. You said you wanted me to make friends here," I say. The clothesline stops moving, and Ramona peeks at me between the pillowcases. "You and Hannah are hitting it off, eh?"

"Sure," I say. "Hannah's pretty cool." It's not a lie, but I'm not sure that Ramona is convinced. I guess I haven't exactly been "Miss Congeniality" since I arrived.

"Well, I guess if you promise t—"

"Great! I knew you'd say yes!" I'm unable to stop myself from smiling.

"Well, well, well. Would you look at that! Izzy Tate knows how to smile."

"Ha ha," I concede. "So, I can go?"

"Yeah. You can go. But give your mom a call. Ask her if it's okay."

"Thanks, Ramona." I push through the wet linen and give her a quick hug. She smells like fabric softener and patchouli and cayenne pepper.

After a quick call to my mom, who gives me the thumbs up to go (yay, Mom!), I run down to my cabin and text Hannah.

It's all good. Orca I is a go.

A text comes back almost immediately: Awesome! Can U B ready by 2?

K. Paddle 2 Mona's when U R ready.

K. Kayak is geared up.

Cool! See u at 2.

C U soon.

At 1:57, I spot Hannah's yellow kayak coming around the point. It doesn't surprise me that she's on time. She just seems like the type. Of course, Jack is there as well, sometimes flying above her head, or a little behind her boat. When she reaches Ramona's dock, Jack is sitting on the bow of the kayak, as if it's the most natural thing in the world for a raven to do.

I reach over for the grab loop near the rear hatch as Hannah tucks into the dock. "Did you do that?" she asks, hopping out expertly, her bare feet leaving two perfect wet prints on the sun-baked wood.

"Do what?"

"The artwork on your kayak." She points to the *Black Swan*, Ramona's kayak, but now with a white enamel design painted from bow to stern on the port side: a tangle of white feathers following the line of the kayak. Like most things I create, I have given it the "Izzy" twist, adding a whole lot of intricate details to the pattern. I'm pretty obsessive-compulsive that way.

"That," Hannah says, "is seriously awesome!"

"Thanks. As far as random doodles go, I guess it doesn't suck that much. And the guy who owns Blue Moon Kayaks in the village was pretty stoked about it, too. He came by earlier to buy some woven placemats from Ramona for his wife."

We do a quick check of our supplies, and go over our plan one more time.

"Listen, are you sure about Max?" I ask again. Boyfriends often mess things up. At least, that's the way it seems to be in my circle of friends. That is, if Cody, Dylan, Marika, Luke and Jess still count as my friends. I've hardly heard from any of them since I left Salt Spring.

"He's good. Don't worry," Hannah assures me.

Max's part in this whole thing is to sleep out in his back yard, where he has promised to keep his eyes fixed on the *Orca I*. If something happens, then he's supposed to alert the world. Personally, I'm not convinced he's going to play by those rules. I think his masculinity is insulted, but as Hannah pointed out, no way would she be allowed on an overnight camping trip with her boyfriend. She has a point.

Ramona comes to the dock and hands me a plastic container.

"Granola bars," she says proudly. "Lots of chocolate in them. Hardly anything healthy."

"Thanks, Ramona," I say, tucking them into my backpack. "And thanks for watching Tango and Oscar and Two-Step for me. I . . . I really appreciate it."

"Don't you worry about them, little Momma," she assures me. "I'm a good Auntie."

"Ready?" Hannah asks as she climbs into her kayak.

"Ready."

Chapter Twenty-Nine

※

HANNAH

I FEEL A PANG OF GUILT as I think about my dad. About how I promised I'd be sensible. But sometimes you have to break a rule or two if there are bigger things at stake. I can't just sit around and do nothing. Dad is all about taking action, and I take after him. He knows that about me.

The shoreline at Skinner Bluff at the base of Mt. Tzouhalem is beautiful. I've been coming here my whole life, usually with Dad in our tandem kayak, or in *Shore Thing*, Ben North's little tender. He likes to drop prawn traps, and there are a lot of prize spots in Sansum Narrows.

But it feels different this time. This time it's not about prawns and rest and relaxation. Not by a long shot.

Izzy and I set up our shelter behind a pile of large rocks. We kill time by making Inukshuks on the rocky beach in front of our little cover, and soon there is an entire slate-made family staring out to sea.

"I hope we can pull this off." I look out at the *Orca I*, listing to one side as it always does, while we sit on an uprooted tree, enjoying Ramona's homemade granola bars. "But we *have* to get on that boat. I seriously hope those dudes aren't around tonight. I sure don't want to get caught."

"You turning chicken?" Izzy asks, chewing slowly.

"Nope. I'm just thinking about the 'what ifs,' you know?"

"Well, don't."

"Maybe you're right." I look up the beach to where Jack is perched on a rock, calmly preening his feathers. Ever since we arrived and pulled our kayaks up into the cove, he seems more like his old self again. Not so uptight.

The afternoon passes slowly. I try to read, but I can't concentrate, so I end up taking way too many photos of rocks and tide pools and close-ups of barnacles that I know I'll delete later when I go to download them.

Izzy, on the other hand, spends hours with her sketchbook and her technical pens, and this time she doesn't mind when I peer over her shoulder.

We whip up a gourmet supper of peanut butter and jam sandwiches along with a thermos of sweet chai tea. Peanut butter, however, was a bad choice: it sticks in my throat and sits like a lump in my over-anxious stomach.

Izzy takes a long swallow of tea and leans her head back to stare up the face of Mt. Tzouhalem. She points to the small speck above a cliff: the huge cross, erected in the '70s, by the Catholic Church.

"So, this is where that badass chief Tzouhalem hung out, eh?"

"Apparently," I tell her. "There are a lot of stories about him and the place. Most of them are pretty disturbing. I've even heard mountain bikers and hikers say that it's haunted."

"Yeah, I know about those stories," Izzy says. "Mom likes to tell that one, too. Especially the part about how someone eventually cut off his head and stuck it on a stick in the village to prove to everyone he was dead." She looks away from the mountain quickly, but I see her sneak a few more looks when she doesn't think I'll notice.

When all the tea is gone and we get tired of talking, I feel myself growing nervous about our risky, middle-of-the-night mission. The water looks black and sinister, and the mountain looms up higher than ever in the dark, like an unfriendly, impenetrable wall.

"I have to pee," I say, and head toward the trees just up from the beach.

"Yeah, me too."

There's nothing around except a dead-end gravel road, and a whole lot of night, but having pretty much lived in the woods that summer I was twelve, squatting in the dark doesn't faze me.

On our way back to the beach, we hear a rustle in the bushes. Instinctively, we both stop.

"Did you hear that?" we whisper together.

The rustling continues, and then we hear footsteps, footsteps that are most definitely getting closer.

"Quick!" I hiss. "Let's get out of here." But we're too late, and as the bushes part, a tall, shadowy figure emerges to block our path. There's no time to be scared. I grab a heavy stick from the ground and raise it over my head.

One . . . two—

"Hannah! It's me! It's Max!"

❧

"You should know me by now," Max says when we're back in the cove, huddled behind a wall of stacked logs. "You actually think I'd let you guys go off by yourselves? I paddled around the point to Genoa Bay after you left and just hung out there for a while."

"But you said you'd keep watch. You said you'd call for help if you heard anything weird out on the water."

"Oh. Right. Like that's really going to be helpful if someone has a knife to your throat. What kind of an idiot do you think I am?"

He's right, of course, maybe over dramatic, but right. We're all here now and maybe it's a good thing—power in numbers and all that.

What if we *do* get into trouble? What if something does happen out there on the water? I shake my head. As Izzy said before, I shouldn't think about the "what if's." No great deeds would ever get done if people worried about what *might* happen. Still, a little caution is not a bad thing. Yet Aunt Maddie and Riley always say to trust your gut, so that's what I'm doing.

But most of all, I trust Jack. There's no way he would lead me here for no reason. He just wouldn't.

Chapter Thirty

AT EXACTLY 2:23 A.M., the three of us take to the water, sliding our kayaks quietly away from the rocky cove. We're wearing our lifejackets under dark sweaters, making us look like CSIS agents gone rogue or something, and while I'm not entirely convinced that this whole covert operation is going to work, I'm not going to lie: I kind of like the look.

The moon is full, and despite the clouds that are moving in, it's not that difficult to see our way to the dark silhouette of the *Orca I* that looms straight ahead. We match each other stroke for stroke, completely in sync, making good time, and when we close in on the *Orca I*, we quit paddling and glide like agile sea ninjas on the glass-like surface of the water.

Although the boat is even bigger than I remember, and even more dark and menacing, there's no glow in any of its windows tonight. That's a good sign.

I shiver in spite of my many layers. The quicker we do this, the better.

"Come on," Hannah says, pushing her kayak forward. "We have to get on board before I can change my mind."

"It's now or never," Max says.

Adrenaline takes over and we paddle to the steel ladder that runs up the hull near the stern.

"Hold this," Hannah mouths, passing her paddle to me. At the same time, I grab hold of the D-ring near the bow of her kayak and watch her limberly pull herself out of her seat and onto the bottom rung of the ladder like a limpet. She climbs stealthily, and quickly disappears over the top onto the deck. A moment later her shape appears, backlit by the moon.

"Piece of cake," she whispers. "Tether the boats to the bottom rung. Let's *do* this!"

Max goes up next, and I follow. My knees are trembling and my hands feel numb and uncooperative as I try to get a good grip on the slippery ladder rungs.

It turns out I'm the biggest hypocrite ever: I'm not so good at taking my own advice. Like ignoring the "what ifs" as Hannah calls them—the what if someone sees us? Or the what if I fall into the icy ocean? And worst of all, the what if someone is sleeping on board?

"Come on, Izzy Tate!" Max hisses at me. "Let's go!" What's with the orders? Who made him boss?

When we're all on deck, Max turns his flashlight on the low beam.

"Are you nuts?" I snatch it from his hand. "You want to light us up for the whole world to see? Wait until we go down into the cabin!"

True to the rumours, the deck *is* covered with pigeon crap, not to mention old bits of rope, tin cans and a few rusted-out oil drums to one side. There are cigarette and cigar butts everywhere, and tons of Big Mountain beer cans piled inside an old truck tire near the cabin door.

We scan the water for any sign of boat traffic, and check the direction of our campsite near Skinner Bluff. No lights. No action. It's all good. All is quiet.

Hannah grabs the handle of the door to the cabin and pulls. "It's locked."

"Great. Now what do we do?"

"Maybe there's another way in. Come on."

We slink single-file along the side of the cabin, and I slip twice on what has to be pigeon crap. But we find a window, a small window, that's open a couple of inches at the bottom.

Max reaches up and grips it firmly. After several tries, it opens.

"Can we fit through that?" Hannah asks. It's a good question: the window looks barely wide enough for a cat to get through. "I'll try," she says. "You guys stay on deck and keep watch."

"That's a stupid idea," Max whispers. "You don't even know what's in there. No way!"

"Listen," Hannah says, "I have to find out. I dragged you guys into this. You both stay at opposite ends of the boat and keep your phones out. Text if anything weird happens, but make sure your phones are on vibrate, okay?"

"Hannah—" but Hannah cuts him off. "Relax, Miller. I'll be fine. Now quit being such an old lady. You're starting to bug me."

"I was just going to say that it might help if you took your life-jacket off."

Smart ass.

Hannah swallows a reply and quickly removes the extra padding. "Okay, give me a leg up would you?"

Max cups his hands together and boosts Hannah to the window. In no time at all her body is through and, with a couple of twists and a grunt, she disappears through the opening. She is sort of scrawny, I guess. Max and I crane our necks to see inside.

The room smells like an armpit: a strong mixture of fish, mold, diesel, cigarettes, rotting wood and something else I can't quite identify, but whatever it is, it's gross.

"Be careful!" I hiss. In the half-light I see her turn to give us a brave thumbs-up.

Then she is gone.

Chapter Thirty-One

❧

HANNAH

WHEN I OPEN THE DOOR at the back of the room, I find myself about to enter a smaller, windowless one. The air inside is thick and when I shine my light across the walls and over the ceiling all I see are cobwebs and mould. The smell is awful.

Focus, Hannah, focus!

It's disgusting, and it's no secret that people have been hanging out here. There are a couple of mattresses and some ratty sleeping bags on the floor, with some newspapers, chip bags and pop bottles filling up the corners. Several big coolers are pushed to one side of the room, and some gumboots and a blue toolbox are in the other, stacked between a pair of big industrial-size deep-freezers.

This isn't the place to lose it if I'm going to finish what I started. I have to keep searching, and take note of every single detail: the water outside, the hum of the muffled generator coming from the other end of the ship, the creak of rotting floorboards, and that smell! A faintly chemical smell hidden somewhere inside the diesel and mold. I hold my sleeve across my nose and try to breathe through the fabric. It smells like something died in here.

I step over a dirty sleeping bag toward one of the freezers. Grabbing hold of the handle, I heave open the lid, which triggers the interior light. I instantly drop the lid, stifling a scream. I steel myself, and slowly open the lid again. It's monstrous—like something out of a horror movie.

The freezer is three-quarters full . . . of animal parts. The first thing I see are paws. Bear paws. They're thrown into a big cardboard box any-which-way, some large, and some much smaller, which obviously belonged to cubs. But it doesn't stop there. There are other things, too. Internal organs of some kind, sealed in zip-loc baggies, stacked haphazardly on the other side of the freezer. Gallbladders. They have to be. That's what one of the newspaper articles said: poachers sell this stuff on the black market for big bucks. The beam from my flashlight catches something in the corner of the room—a pile of burlap sacks. I walk over and open one of them, clutching at my stomach to stop it from heaving.

It is surreal. The sack is full of antlers. Most of them broken in pieces, but there are lots of them. Probably elk, from the Roosevelt elk that live on the Island. Someone is harvesting the velvet. Some skin still clings to some of the pieces—the source of the foul stench!

I can't stand it. The sight of so much senseless killing and the accompanying smell makes me queasy. I force back tears, and turn a full circle, unsure of where to look, trying to get a grip.

Come on, Hannah! Snap out of it!

I walk over to the other freezer, flip the lid, and look inside. What I see will stay with me forever. Inside this freezer are at least fifteen bald eagle carcasses—adult birds, frozen solid, their talons and beaks removed. Each one is individually wrapped in a clear plastic bag, tossed carelessly inside the freezer like so much garbage. I place a hand on one of the bags and shiver, not from the cold. I wonder if I'm looking at Two-Step's mate: at Tango and Oscar's mother. What *is* this place? What kind of sicko would do this?

Then I remember my phone. I have to get photos of this. Evidence! But I have to hurry.

While I'm digging in my pocket for it, it pings and the screen lights up. A text from Izzy.

Get out! Someone is coming!

If I'm going to get photos, there's no time to answer her.

Another text comes in: Han! now! gtg!

I rush back through the door to the first room and hear

frantic movement outside the window that I crawled through. A moment later I hear splashing from the water below. Of course. The kayaks. They'll stand out like a sore thumb!

I shove my phone deep into my pocket to silence it. I can hear men's voices out on the water, and the sound of an approaching motor. I stick my head through the open window and strain to see over the few feet of deck and down to the water. Sure enough, I spot the tail end of the *Black Swan* bobbing below.

"Izzy!" I hiss. "You have to go . . . NOW!"

"HANNAH!" The *Black Swan* comes into full view—and the shape of Izzy as she points her hand toward the sound of the approaching tender.

"Just go! And take my kayak, too. If they see the kayaks, we're doomed. I'll be fine. I'll hide. GO! NOW!"

I haven't felt this full of adrenaline and determination since Tl'ulpalus. Not since the chase in the forest with Yisella when we ran from the Thumquas. Well, I survived then, and I'll survive now. If I could do that, I can do this. I am *not* leaving without proof!

I pull my head in from the window, run back to the adjoining room and, once inside, grope blindly around in the darkness for the freezers. Thankfully the room is small and the freezers are big, but I still manage to trip over a mattress and fall to my knees.

I find a freezer, flip open the lid exposing the horror inside, and snap off four photos on my phone. Next I turn and shoot a rapid-fire series of shots at the pile of antlers in the corner.

I hear the motor of the approaching tender sputter and die near the boat. I probably have less than a minute before things could go really, really wrong.

There isn't time to get to the other freezer—the one with the eagles—but I have enough, enough evidence to show the police. It's *got* to be enough. I race to the front room and hunker down beneath the partially open window, because I can't think of anywhere else to go. Maybe whoever is out there won't come on board. Maybe they—

I hear men's voices, and when I hear someone's footsteps at the other end of the ship, I pray for a miracle, anything to buy me just a little more time—just one more minute.

"Damn it, there's no juice in this flashlight!" The voice is close. "I can't see my hand in front of my goddamn face."

My miracle! Thank you, universe! I don't dare move, even though my leg is cramping up.

"For Christ's sake, Buzz, go get the other flashlight from the front of the tender then!" I recognize this other voice right away. *Kelso.*

I can't stand it. I slowly stand up and look out the window, just in time to see the two dark, ghostly shapes of Max and Izzy tucked in behind the floating buoy a little way out on the water.

I turn my head to see a dim light appear in a room at the other end of the ship, and a shadow flickers past the glass. That must be where the generator is kept. Moments later, the light disappears and when I duck down, I hear footsteps on the deck again, coming closer. I sit like a statue beneath the window ledge.

"Wish we coulda waited a couple more days." A voice says. "Would have been nice to nab a couple more yogi bears."

"Forget it, Kelso! Webber's dope deal goes down tomorrow. We gotta wrap this up tonight. The guy is paying good coin for these critters, so let's get moving."

"Chill out, Buzz. Don't get twisted. It all worked out!"

My leg is cramping up again but I don't dare move. I can hear both men clear as day, right on the other side of the half-open window.

Please go away! Please go away! Please go away!

"We're not home-free, yet," Buzz says. "Not until—"

"Hey!" Kelso interrupts, and I hear some shuffling near the window. "What's this? Where did this life-jacket come from?"

I press myself against the wall, holding my breath.

"You leave this window open, dumbass?"

I move to one side and hold my breath, but moments later the locked steel door bangs open and I am yanked to my feet so roughly that I pitch forward and smash my knees on the cement floor.

"Well, would ya look at this—a stowaway!" It's Kelso. He pushes his face in close to mine, gripping my jacket with both hands. "Looking for something, kid?"

His breath is awful: a blend of chicken manure, coffee and cigarettes, and my stomach lurches as I stagger back and turn my face away. "I . . . I got lost. My boat tipped. I . . . I—"

"Where's your boat now?" Kelso hauls me back through the open door and out onto the deck, gripping my shoulders tight in his meaty hands. My knees burn, and I gasp out loud.

"It . . . it sank!"

"Well now, isn't that unfortunate," Kelso says. "Imagine that." Buzz stands in front of us, laughing like a maniac while he shakes a finger in my face.

"Good thing we're here to rescue you, eh?" he snickers.

I look away, discreetly checking for Izzy and Max out on the water, but there is no sign of them. My only hope is that they are on their way to Genoa Bay for help. Still, how did they get away so fast?

"Hey!" Kelso says, catching my eye. "What are you looking at? Someone out there?" In a blur he is across the deck, over the railing and down the ladder, leaving me in the hands of the scrawny, yet surprisingly strong Buzz. There is a scuffle and some swearing, and when he reappears with a terrified-looking Max, holding what looks like a gun at the small of Max's back, I forget to breathe. "Buzz! There's another kid out there! I can see the kayak!"

Buzz shoves me at Kelso and then he's gone. I hear the tender start up and race away from the ship. A few seconds later, the motor dies and someone screams: a girl.

Izzy!

Chapter Thirty-Two

❦

IZZY

WHY DID I LISTEN TO MAX? Why did I let him go back to the *Orca I* for Hannah? We should have *both* gone straight for help. But when I think about Hannah, I can see Max is right. Would I want everyone to ditch me if I was trapped up on that deck?

I point my kayak toward the black open water, towing Hannah's kayak behind me, as Max fades into the dark in the opposite direction, back to the *Orca I*.

I paddle like I've never paddled before, heading for the darkest part of the water before I can horseshoe back to the marina for help.

But I'm too late. I hear an outboard motor start up, and in less than a minute a big orange tender is up alongside my kayak. I barely have time to register what's happening as a powerful pair of hands reaches across and grabs the cockpit rim so hard that my vessel almost turns right over.

"Get in. NOW!" The man in the tender shakes my kayak, and when I freeze, he says, "Hard of hearing, kid? I said get in the tender now! And if I were you, I'd do it."

I don't argue. Instead, I lift myself out of the cockpit with trembling legs, as the man grabs hold of my sweater and pulls me roughly into the boat beside him.

"Stupid kids," he says under his breath, as we head back to the *Orca I*. "You're a bunch of stupid, stupid kids."

❧

"Not a word out of any of you!" Kelso warns, as the three of us huddle together on the deck.

"Hand over your phones!" says the guy with the tatts—Buzz—gesturing to our pockets with one of his bony hands. "I know you got some. Now!"

"I can't," Hannah says. "I lost mine somewhere on the boat."

"Find her phone," Kelso says to Buzz, and then looks to Max. "Don't just sit there, kid. You deaf? Phones. Hand them over."

Max and I hand over our phones and, without hesitation, Kelso fires them both straight out into the water where they sink like stones. This isn't good. This isn't good at all.

"You!" Kelso says to me. He grabs my arm and yanks me to my feet. Max lunges forward suddenly, pushing him several feet across the deck.

But Kelso is stronger than he looks.

"Oh, ya think so?" he says hotly, grabbing for Max.

He brings his face up close to Max's. "You think you're a tough guy, kid? You sure you can take us? Is that what you think?"

Max doesn't break eye contact. "What I think, is that you oughta buy some mouthwash, dude."

Kelso brings his fist up but Buzz grabs his wrist. "Kelso, don't be an ass! He's a frikkin' kid!"

Kelso hesitates, and then swears. He throws Max down on the other side of Hannah as though he's a sack of potatoes. I see him wince.

"If any of you are thinking of trying anything? Think again!"

Buzz turns to head back into the room, but Kelso stays. "You open your mouths, the fun's over, you got that, Red?" he says, looking straight at Hannah. "And you," he points to Max, "don't be a hero."

"Those kids aren't going any place," Buzz calls over his shoulder. "Leave 'em alone! Quit wasting time! We have to move out the critter parts and clean up before tomorrow night. We don't have a lot of time. Shit, if Webber ever finds out what we've been up—"

"Relax," Kelso snorts. "As far as Ray knows, this ship's cargo is weed. End of story. He's never set foot near the freezer room. Only been here twice, both times to check on the weed. Probably doesn't like gettin' them Italian designer shoes dirty." He coughs and spits onto the deck. "And you 'n' me? Why, we're just a couple of hardworking employees, workin' hard for our cut." He laughs and kicks Max's foot hard. "Don't even *think* about moving," he says acidly. "We'll all get better acquainted later."

We sit there, watching helplessly as Buzz and Kelso walk back and forth in front of us, loading the packages from the freezer room onto the deck. They are quick and silent—real pros. When they go back for the burlap sacks of elk antlers, I know our time is running out. We have to do something!

Hannah leans in close to us and hisses, "Max, do you still have your Maglite?"

"What? Why!"

"Seriously. Just give it to me!"

He digs into his pocket and hands it to her, but I think she might be losing it. After all, what good is a flashlight going to be in our current predicament?

"Cover me," she whispers to Max and me. "This just might work!"

Chapter Thirty-Three

❦

HANNAH

I DON'T KNOW WHY IT comes to me out of the blue—the conversation I'd had with Ben North that morning on the dock—but in a flash I remember all of it.

"What are you doing? Trying to scare the fish?" I'd asked him.

"An SOS." Ben had chuckled. "I'm calling for help. Cranky teenage girls scare me."

I love you, Ben North!

Three short bursts of light, then three longer ones, followed by three short. An SOS! It's worth a shot. It's all we have.

When Buzz and Kelso go back into the dark freezer room, I spring into action.

"Go!" Max whispers. "Go, go, go, *go!*"

I shine the high-powered flashlight directly at the marina, right where I think Riley and the *Tzinquaw* are anchored. Riley never sleeps. Everyone in the bay knows that. If he isn't out fishing, he's almost always on his deck, whittling away at something, or hanging out with Ben and Sadie.

"Hurry!" Izzy whispers.

Three short bursts of light. That part is easy. The three longer ones are harder to get right. It's not easy to slow down when your heart rate has speeded up, and your hands are shaking. But I have to get it right. I have to. I finish with three quick flashes. Then comes the hardest part of all, the excruciating five-second pause: *one—two—three—four—five.* And then, repeat.

"Stop!" Max says, yanking my sleeve. "They're coming back."

I sit back down, dropping my hand to the deck, which is slimy with pigeon crap. Gross.

Stay focused, Hannah.

It's Aunt Maddie's favourite word: focus. Breathe in. Breathe out. Don't lose it. Be slow and steady. *Focus!*

"Me and my buddy here are gonna take a little trip up the narrows in the tender," Kelso tells us when the last of the "cargo" sits waiting on the deck. "Too bad we don't have room for you three. Get up." He grabs hold of Max and spins him around as Buzz pulls Izzy and me to our feet.

"Well, we can't shoot you," Kelso grins, "so guess we're gonna have to lock you up for a while. Now march." Buzz climbs onto the deck from the ladder and the two men shove us into the freezer room. "And no one get any ideas about leaving any time soon," Buzz says. "You stay put and nothing bad will happen. You got it? Just sit still and shut up." He motions for us to sit on the floor, and we do.

"Where are you guys going?" Max asks bluntly.

"None of your damn business, kid," Kelso answers.

Buzz clears his throat and spits out the door. "Better tie them up, Kelso. Or else the scrawny ones will be through that window the minute we're gone."

"What do you think the rope is for, dumbass," Kelso says, holding up a coil of thick blue cord in his right hand.

The two men share a laugh, and Buzz removes a joint from his shirt pocket. He lights it up, inhaling long and hard. "*Ahhhhhhh*, a little BC bud to warm the soul." He coughs twice, before passing the joint to Kelso.

They are so intent on passing the joint back and forth that they don't hear a boat approaching. But Izzy, Max and I do. We stare at each other, and then at Buzz and Kelso, who are oblivious to everything except the glowing ember in the space between them.

Oh, please. Oh, please. Oh, please. Has help arrived?

But instead of "help" appearing, an angry voice breaks the silence, out on the deck. "Goddamnit!" it barks. "What the hell *is* all this?"

Kelso sucks in his breath so fast, he inhales the joint, which hits the back of his throat, then shoots out of his mouth in a shower of sparks. I can almost feel Kelso's face turning purple. Buzz jumps about a foot in the air, and the two of them are out through the door in a blur. The joint butt fizzles and dies on the damp concrete of the floor.

"KELSO? BUZZ?" the voice yells, "What are you doing on the *Orca I*? Job goes down tomorrow, not tonight!"

I can't believe it. I know that voice. It's Sabrina's uncle. Ray Webber!

"What the hell's going on with that tender?" he hisses.

Max and Izzy and I look at each other and instantly race through the open door to take refuge behind a suspended dinghy on the deck. We hunker down low, and I hold my index finger in front of my lips. We have to think this out. We have to be smart. No rash moves.

But still, the danger surrounding us is so much bigger than three teenagers are fit to take on. How did we end up this way? Why didn't I just go to the police with my suspicions? Why didn't I tell Riley, or Ben, or Nell, or Aunt Maddie? Why did I think I could solve this on my own? And what are the odds of anyone seeing my SOS?

I think about Dad. It would be mid-morning in Spain. He's probably eating some bread and fruit and having his third cup of coffee and chatting with local villagers. It's all so surreal. Will I ever see him again? Is this how it ends?

Something passes between us in the space between the dinghy and the side of the ship with a wild *swooooosh*, brushing close by my cheek. I stifle a gasp as the dark shape lands in front of my feet, wings folding, and ruffled ever so slightly. It's Jack!

Max and Izzy are as surprised as I am. None of us say a word as he flies up and settles on top of the radio antenna. I have never been happier to see anyone or anything. I know it's stupid. I can't explain it. I know a raven can't save three people from impending doom, but Jack's arrival makes me feel so much better. I can't put it into words but it's about the connection. It's about our history.

I reach up to touch the abalone around my neck.

"*It will help to keep you safe*," Yisella had said when she'd given it to me. I close my eyes, and think of her. I think of her strong chin, and the quick and careful steps she took on the trail when she had a destination in mind. I remember her fearlessness, and how stubborn she could be when she made up her mind to do something. But what I remember most of all was her resolve to do the right thing. No matter what the cost. Always. Thinking about her and seeing Jack up on the antenna fills me with hope. We are not supposed to end our lives out here . . . on a boat stowed with pot and animal parts! What would be the point?

I can hear Ray Webber tearing a strip off Kelso and Buzz. Did he even see us? Does he know we're here?

And then all three men are talking at once.

"Damn it! Someone else is out there!"

"Jesus! I see it!"

"Headed straight for us!"

"We gotta move this tub!"

I see Buzz make a run for the engine room at the far end of the deck. Soon, all other sounds are drowned out by the sound of the *Orca I*'s heavy diesel engine groaning to life. It rumbles, low and long, shaking the deck with the intensity of a passing freight train, coughing and sputtering while smoke billows from the engine room, filling the air around us.

But a bright flash of light cuts through the smoke, and sends Jack into a power dive off the radio antenna and out over the sea. Someone *is* out there! I shield my eyes against the brightness, run to the *Orca I*'s railing, and wave my arms frantically at the vessel heading toward us.

"I knew it!" I yell at the top of my lungs, unable to contain my excitement. "I knew it!" I'd recognize that beat-up cabin anywhere: the painted wing on the side of the weathered wood. Riley!

"It's the *Tzinquaw*!" Max and Izzy shout together, joining me at the railing. "It's Riley!"

I am dizzy with relief. He saw it! He saw my SOS. I should have known. I laugh out loud as the sound of the *Tzinquaw*'s straining motor fills the air.

Riley raises a hand to signal back, but before I can shout to him, I feel a grip on my shoulder and someone pulls me backwards.

"Thought I told you and your friends to stay put, Red?" Kelso shoves me against the side of the boat, and my back makes contact with a big metal rivet that sends a stabbing pain down my side.

"Hey!" Max yells, "Get your greasy hands off her!" He lunges forward and slams a fist forcefully into the side of Kelso's face, knocking him backwards through the filth to land hard against an oil barrel.

Jack drops from the sky and arcs past me, headed straight for Kelso, who ducks at the last minute, again losing his footing.

"Max!" I call to him as he jumps to the top of a raised platform near the ladder. He reaches for a plank of wood lying on top, but Kelso is faster, and gets to it first.

"MAX!"

Time seems to stop, and then Kelso raises the plank, poised like a batter at the plate, ready to take a swing at Max's head!

Chapter Thirty-Four

✤

IZZY

THE *TZINQUAW* REVS HARD and lurches sideways, almost slamming into the huge metal side of the *Orca I*. While Kelso is distracted by the vessel Hannah runs straight at him, shoving him hard into the railing. He drops the board, which skitters awkwardly across the deck.

In a sudden burst of speed, the *Tzinquaw* surges ahead as the *Orca I* regains equilibrium and levels out again. Riley pushes his boat's engine to the limit, gunning it forward in full throttle. With a final thrust, he is in front of us and, seconds later, appears at the stern of his boat. He moves fast, ducking and reaching and lifting—pitching things off the back of the boat that hit the water in a rapid succession of massive splashes.

Seconds later, the *Orca I*'s engine squeals and grinds to a stop with an earsplitting, metal-on-metal sound. It lists hard to one side, and then pitches forward at the bow. Kelso stumbles, and hovers on one foot for a moment before pitching straight over the railing and into the water.

Buzz and Ray Webber burst out of the engine room followed by a cloud of thick smoke.

"Man overboard!"

From somewhere over my head, I hear Jack calling.

Chaos is everywhere.

❦

The female RCMP officer has a calming voice. "You sure none of you kids are hurt?"

None of us can speak. At least not right away.

"We're okay," Hannah tells her for all of us. "We're fine."

While Buzz, Ray Webber and Kelso are cuffed and held on the *Orca I* until the police boat dispatched from Mill Bay arrives, Hannah, Max and I are quickly hustled onto a Coast Guard Auxiliary cutter.

Half an hour later the three of us sit with mugs of hot chocolate in our hands, and blankets draped round our shoulders, while a medic takes our vital signs.

Riley sits hunched on a chair across from us, a thick blanket thrown around his angular, bony shoulders. His clothing is soaked, but his eyes are alert and intense.

"Come on, old man. What happened out here?" The other police office, Constable Carr, asks, handing him a mug.

Riley shifts, and lets the female police officer tend to the cut on his hand. "I saw Hannah's SOS out on the water. I'm not much of a sleeper. Thought it was just a bunch of partiers on a boat fooling around, but I called 9-1-1 anyway, and when I got closer and saw it was coming from the *Orca I*, my antenna went up." Riley stops to take a sip from the mug of hot chocolate in his now bandaged hand. "I saw Hannah right away. And then I saw someone about to take a strike at young Mr. Miller here. I wasn't about to sit back and wait for help, you know? It was a long shot, but I figured if I dropped everything I had in her path—you know, mooring lines, nets, gear —well, it just might seize the prop of the *Orca I*. Ol' *Tzinquaw* and I have seen a lot of things out on the water. I was pretty sure she wouldn't let me down."

"Impulsive," the female officer, Constable Drake, says, "but good thing we happened to be close by when we got the 9-1-1 call."

Hannah, Max and I exchange looks, finally realizing just how out of our depth we'd actually been. None of us say anything but we clasp our hands together, squeezing hard.

Somewhere out on the water, an eagle cries.

Chapter Thirty-Five

❦

HANNAH

DERELICT *ORCA I* COVER-UP FOR
POACHING & DRUG SMUGGLING OPERATION

I READ EVERY SINGLE word of the article twice, and then once more for good measure. Kelso, it seems, is part of an organized poaching ring that, among other things, has been harvesting abalone up around Bamfield for quite some time. What a loser.

Buzz had a prior record, for possession of marijuana mostly, and it isn't really clear how he got mixed up with Kelso and the animal poaching.

But it's Sabrina's uncle Ray that is the real surprise. Mr. "Salt-of-the-Earth." The guy that almost everyone thought was so solid. I *knew* there was something off about him. I just knew it.

I turn the page, reading about how when the *Orca I* was seized, they uncovered 1,200 pounds of pot, all packaged up and hidden in the ship's boiler room! The newspaper says it would have been worth over a million dollars on the street. A million dollars! All from pot grown just north of here. And the dollar figure is almost as high for the poached animal parts.

Then I reread the final paragraph. The one that makes me smile:

> Although they put themselves in great danger, three local teens, Hannah Anderson, Isabelle Tate, and Max Miller, were instrumental in uncovering the operation. Although they were in great danger, these young people showed remarkable fortitude and determination.
>
> "I was scared," remarked fourteen-year-old Hannah Anderson, when local RCMP recently spoke with the gutsy teens. "But we had to stop them. I just kept thinking about the animals that live here. How I had to protect them. That kept us going."

My phone rings as I'm studying the image in the centre of the text: a half-page, colour photo of the *Orca I*, taken when they towed it out of the bay. There's a "not-so-mysterious" black raven perched on its radio antenna. Big surprise.

"Did you read the paper yet?" Izzy asks breathlessly when I answer my phone.

"Only about a million times," I tell her.

"Can you believe it? Can you believe we actually nailed those guys?"

"I know. I'm going to be in so much trouble with my dad when he gets back from Spain. Not to mention that I think my aunt is going to duct tape me to the kitchen chair now until school starts." It's true, and while Aunt Maddie is an activist at heart, my being escorted home by two police officers just before dawn did very little to impress her.

"I know what you mean," Izzy says. "Did you know my mom is here?"

"She is?"

"Yeah, go figure. It's totally out of character, but she arrived practically a nano-second after I got to Ramona's. My little sister is here, too."

"Amelia?"

"Yeah. And I have to keep telling her the whole story over and over again. Every. Single. Detail."

"Well, it *is* a pretty cool story."

"I *know*. I still can't believe it." Izzy's voice softens. "My mom told her an old Cowichan legend. Do you know the one about Thunderbird—the *Tzinquaw*—and the monster orca?"

"Yeah," I say. "I know that one. Ben told it to me."

"I haven't thought about that legend for years," Izzy says. "I think I remember my mom telling it to me when I was little. When I was Amelia's age. Even before my dad left."

"Ha! Guess you were listening to those stories after all," I suggest.

"Maybe you're right."

"And that one *is* pretty special, don't you think?" I say. "You know, given the recent circumstances and everything."

Izzy laughs. A real laugh, like she means it. "You have a point," she says. And then adds, "Hey! The cops brought the kayaks back this morning! They're all here. No damage or anything. They were just floating around out there with no place to go."

"Really? That's great!" During all the chaos, the kayaks had been the least of my worries, but now that they're back, I'm so glad.

I hear noise in the background, followed by muffled voices, and then a little kid's voice, loud and clear.

"Izzy! You *have* to come outside right this very second!"

"Why?" I hear Izzy say.

"Because Tango flew! I was looking for crabs on the beach and I heard a sound so I looked up and saw Tango on the branch and then he squawked and he flew over the water. He did! I saw him! And he did really, really *SO* good, too! Come and see, Izzy! Come right now!"

"You hear that, Hannah? Did you hear Amelia? Tango fledged!"

"I'm on my way!"

I turn to see Aunt Maddie, leaning against the fridge, her arms folded in front of her, trying her best to play the stern disciplinarian. "What's up?"

"Tango flew! I have to go!"

She softens immediately. "Well, what are we waiting for?"

"Okay, then," I say. "Get your shoes on! Let's go!"

⁂

When Aunt Maddie pulls over to the gravel verge in front of the Salish Sea Studio, I'm out of the jeep before it comes to a full stop. I race down the side of the house, turn the corner sharply, narrowly missing running into a patch of tall, pink delphiniums.

Izzy, Max and Ramona are already on the dock, along with a dark-haired woman and a little girl of about seven: Izzy's mom and sister. There are a lot of squeals and pointing, and sure enough, when we join them, the distinctive mottled brown and white wings of Tango are gliding over the surface of the water, strong and confident. Higher up, Two-Step watches like the proud father he is, intent and focused.

"Look!" Amelia says, turning around and pointing up to the nest. "Oscar is on the branch. He's flapping! Izzy, is he going to fly too?"

We watch as Oscar takes a few tentative steps along the branch to a clear spot, and then begins flapping his wings. He does this softly at first, then with more and more energy. He stops and starts, building momentum, but doesn't really move.

"What's he doing?" Amelia asks.

"Practising," Izzy tells her. Oscar has always been the more cautious of the two birds. Maybe he just needs a little more time.

After a five-minute rest, he starts up again, beating his wings furiously, hopping carefully out to the farthest edge of the branch.

"Come on, Oscar!" Amelia claps. "You can do it!"

I cross my fingers on both hands behind my back.

I look over at Izzy, and her eyes, so much like Yisella's, are closed in deep concentration as she whispers under her breath, "Just a little further out, buddy. You can do it. Just one little hop and you're in the air."

As if he's listening, Oscar looks at her and launches himself into the air. His beautiful wings, slightly paler than Tango's, stretch out as he flies between the branches, dropping, recovering, and then swooping down between two trunks. He hesitates and then rises up again to burst through the tangle of limbs.

We cheer him on as he meets up with his brother, and the pair of them cut through the cloudless blue sky as though they've been flying forever.

I get a big lump in my throat as I watch them, feeling so grateful that they made it this far. I look over to Izzy to see that her eyes are wet as she follows the bird's flight path above our heads.

Two-Step doesn't move or make any sort of sound at all from his perch in his tree. He just watches, patient and hopeful, trusting that they'll get it right and find their way. Two-Step, I decide, is a very good single parent.

Izzy's mother grabs hold of her daughter's hand. "It's hard watching your babies grow up, isn't it?"

"They're not my babies, Mom," Izzy says quietly, but there's no anger in her voice.

"Well, you've been watching them grow. Feeding them. Keeping them safe. Sure sounds like motherhood to me."

"They'll be fine. They know what to do now. They don't need me anymore." But there is a catch in Izzy's voice.

Mrs. Tate's face softens. "Take some credit, Izzy. You did a really great thing for those birds. You took them on. You should feel good about that."

"Don't be so dramatic, Ma. It was nothing."

Mrs. Tate smiles. "So bull-headed. So much like Taatka."

Izzy whirls around to stare at her. "Taatka?"

"You know the story, don't you?" her mom says with a wink, sneaking a glance at Ramona.

"Sort of."

"Hmmmm," Mrs. Tate says. "I thought as much."

Izzy shields her eyes with both hands and gazes out to sea, trying to find her eagles again.

I remember how she was the day I first met her. How fierce. Determined to do the right thing. So much like Yisella was . . .

I watch Tango and Oscar fly side-by-side, right over our heads. The smile on Izzy's face is Yisella's smile, and it has survived all these years.

Chapter Thirty-Six

I'M PRETTY SURE THE entire population of Cowichan Bay is congregated on Ramona's back lawn. Riley and Ben are seated near the textiles shack, arguing about illegal rock cod catches, while Bea and Art from the Salty Dog Café are playing a mean game of badminton with an elderly couple staying at the Old Rose B&B next door. Most of the houseboat people are sprawled on blankets on the grass that slopes down to the water.

I catch a whiff of someone's cigarette—probably Ben's—and feel pretty proud of myself. I haven't smoked for weeks. And strangely enough, I don't even miss it. Not even a little. Yay, me!

At the water's edge, Nell and Hannah toss a ball for Quincy, who keeps shaking himself off in front of Hannah's aunt, and Max's parents help my mom and Ramona bring the food outside. As usual, my mom is laughing; she's joking with Max's mom about something. She's wearing a light green dress and has kicked off her shoes. She looks, I dunno. Good. Less frantic, somehow.

She's been pretty cool since the whole *Orca I* thing. She didn't even interrupt me when the police came over to interview Max and Hannah and me beneath Two-Step's tree. She even showed the cops my drawings of Tango and Oscar. They're going to use them in an article the newspaper is running on poaching!

The sun is warm and golden, and I hold my face up to it before I go to get some salad and smoked salmon from the buffet table.

"Well, there you go," Scott Hancock, the owner of Blue Moon Kayaks says as I place food on my plate. "That's the work of a true artist."

"Pardon me?"

"Your plate. Such a beautiful presentation," he kids. "The tomato. The cucumber. Complementary colours. It's all there."

I laugh.

"Listen, Izzy," he says, taking a roll from a wicker basket on the table. "It was really good to meet you when I came here to buy my wife the placemats awhile back. I sure am a big fan of what you did on the *Black Swan* out there. I was just wondering . . . do you think you might be interested in doing something similar on my fleet of kayaks?"

I put my knife and fork down on the side of my plate. "Seriously?"

"Yeah," he says, "a part-time job. After school in September, that kind of thing."

I look up from my plate to see Mom standing a few feet away, beaming at me as if I'm some kind of celebrity. She must have already told people that we're moving in with Ramona at the end of the month. Yeah, I know. If someone had asked me a few weeks ago how I'd feel about such a plan, I definitely would have had something to say about it! It's funny how things can change.

"So," Scott says, "what do you think?"

I give him the thumbs up. "I think . . . yes."

Chapter Thirty-Seven

HANNAH

AFTER THE PARTY WINDS down at Ramona's, Max and I decide to take a little walk together.

"I found my diary," I tell him sheepishly when we get to the trailhead in the woods. "You know, the one I thought I was missing?"

I feel like a dork, because it had dropped from my closet shelf while I'd been looking for my yearbook, to land with a smack on my foot. I have a bruised big toe to show for it.

"So Sabrina never took it?" Max asks, slowing down a little.

"I guess not," I say, "but I still don't know how she knew all that stuff."

Max nods, but he doesn't say anything.

"I mean, I took it to school a couple times. I guess she could have read it then. I dunno."

"Are you going to call her on it?"

"Maybe," I say. "No. I don't know."

"I guess she must be feeling seriously crappy right now. You know, having a drug smuggler for an uncle, and—"

"Yeah," I cut in. I want to change the subject. I want to put it—*everything*—behind me. "Hey!" I say. "Let's go . . . you know . . . there!"

❧

The site is unchanged. The same thick tangle of blackberry brambles, salal, and bracken fern conceal the cave. The light is the same, and the quiet stillness is just as it always was.

As I stand on the trail, I can't help feeling as though no time has passed at all since I first shimmied under the tangle of brush to find the cave's narrow opening.

"Doesn't seem like very long ago, does it?" Max says, taking my hand.

"No," I say. "It feels like yesterday."

Everything looks the same except that we can't get to the entrance anymore. It's now an official protected site.

"I knew back then you were a pretty amazing girl, you know," Max says.

"You did?"

"Yeah. You were just so fearless. I'd never met anyone like you."

He pats the space between us and I inch a little closer, feeling, oddly, a bit shy. He brushes my hair away from my face. "This could be a perfect kissing moment, don't you think?" He points to the sunlight spilling through the ferns and onto the trail, and then to Jack, who is so obviously spying on us from a nearby cedar tree.

Max smiles, and moves in for the kiss.

"Wow," I say when it's over. "That was totally a movie star kiss."

"It was," he agrees. "Want to try another one? I think I need the practice."

"I don't think you need any practice at all," I tell him, "but who am I to stand in the way of your education."

As afternoons go, this one rates right up there.

❧

"Come on, Han," Aunt Maddie says on the way to the airport to pick up Dad. "Let's go to a different restaurant tonight. Change it up a little?"

"No way," I tell her. "Figaro's."

"But you guys *always* go there!"

"Yep," I agree. "Ever since I've been old enough to hold my own fork."

"Come on, try something different, Hannah. Live on the edge."

I laugh out loud. "Um . . . I think I've had enough living on the edge for a while," I say, which is completely true.

"So, I can't convince you to try the Beat Street Café tonight?" Aunt Maddie asks. "It's pretty trendy. Great place for young people, I hear."

"Nope." I stick to my decision, and an hour later the three of us, Dad, Aunt Maddie and I, are settled into a corner booth at Figaro's. It's our favourite—the one beneath the bright acrylic painting of a bunch of apples on a black-and-white-checkered tablecloth. I sink back against the red vinyl with a triumphant smile.

"Okay, okay," Aunt Maddie says, rolling her eyes. "I surrender. I have to admit, Fig's is a pretty nice place to be."

"Told you so!" Dad and I say in unison.

My father's eyes are bright and lively. Aunt Maddie tells him he looks tanned and fit, and that his hair, or what's left of it, looks great when it's a little bleached out.

He spends a good two hours telling us about the trials and tribulations of trekking the Camino de Santiago trail. He tells us about the people he met (exaggerating, I'm sure), the villages along the way, the food he ate, the wine he drank, and only stops long enough to show us photographs that correspond to the story. He says his book is going to practically write itself, and that his publisher won't believe it when he gets the first draft done in only three months. His intentions are admirable, so Aunt Maddie and I just smile in a totally supportive sort of way. He always figures it will only take three months to write whatever book he's working on. It's always the same. "Three" seems to be the magic number. Never mind that it usually takes him three *times* that much time to churn out just his first draft.

Aunt Maddie and I nod as if we totally get it, but sneak each other secret glances when he turns his attention to his mocha-swirl cheesecake.

Later, as we chug up the Malahat headed for home, I sink into a kind of post-sugar, endorphin-filled heaven in the backseat. If things are back to normal, then *normal* feels pretty awesome.

By the time we reach the Malahat's summit, the car is quiet —my dad's chatter now replaced by steady deep breathing that tells me he's fallen asleep. It makes me realize how much I missed him while he was gone. I have no idea how I'm going to tell him about everything that's happened since he's been away. I guess I'll just have to start at the beginning, and go from there. There will be lots of time for swapping stories in the days to come.

But for now, this quiet moment is perfect, and I stare out the window at the moon lighting up the Salish Sea.

ABOUT THE AUTHOR

CAROL ANNE SHAW is a writer and artist living in Cobble hill on Vancouver Island. She has lived on her two-acre rural paradise for the past twenty years, along with her artist husband Richard and their two dogs, Eddie and Ruby. Their two grown sons, both in their twenties, also live on the island.

In her younger days, Carol Anne tried her hand at many different jobs: everything from driving a front-end loader, to bartending, to working on a dude ranch, to operating a travelling bookmobile. Eventually she found herself at art school, and now works part-time in the art department of a private boarding school. Not only does she get to be messy and creative, she has the opportunity to assist young evolving artists on their own creative journeys. In return, her students' conversations have provided inspiration for the characters in her novels.

Her debut novel, *Hannah & the Spindle Whorl*, quickly became a success with middle-grade readers (also with many adults), and led to *Hannah & the Salish Sea*. Presently, Carol Anne is hard at work on the final book of the trilogy, *Hannah & the Wild Woods*. Please visit her at her website: www.carolanneshaw.com.